LINDA MCKOWN

I0550433

# RAIMENT RED

# AND

# A RAVEN

## A SOUTHWEST MYSTERY

## BY

## LINDA MCKOWN

Publisher LindaMcKownAuthor LLC
Scottsdale, AZ

# RAIMENT RED AND A RAVEN

RAIMENT RED AND A RAVEN

ISBN-13: 978-0-9997357-8-7

Library of Congress Control Number: 2019908848

(Former LLCN 2019902718, ISBN 978-0-9997357-6-3)

Author:
LindaMcKownAuthor LLC
11574 E Running Deer Trail
Scottsdale, AZ 85262
https://www.lindamckown.com

Any names of people and entities are fictitious in this story having been created by the author's imagination.

Front Cover Photo of the book was purchased from Shutterstock. Book title manipulation was done by Joseph McKown

## LINDA MCKOWN

This book was written for all the wonderful bird species in their wild habitats. This author acknowledges their beauty, mystique, and presence in our lives.

Thank you to my family for encouraging me to continue to write.

# Contents

# 1 Photo Shoot with a Raven

**Ali Zarin was** excited about her opportunity to pose for a cover on one of the largest women's magazines in the United States called Star Magazine. She did prior photography shoots for magazines as a model in college and afterwards. The only thing different was those articles were small and photos insignificant. The photo shoot would coincide nicely with her promotion at KMDZ-LA10 as manager of the Los Angeles news.

This opportunity was what she worked for her whole life. Dreams did come true for a person who worked hard. She worked 24/7 and earned this new exciting chance. No one gave this job to her. She did lean heavily on a friend's influence in the news industry. Lisa Givens knew the CEO, Mr. Fleming.

The location for the photo shoot was at a private, rented home outside of Aspen, Colorado. The lodge was bustling with skiers and their families. The ski runs and restaurants were full at night.

The film crew arrived. The props person deposited her gown in the bedroom. Her full length, designer red crimson dress was wrapped in a plastic white bag. The dress was a princess style design with silver threads interwoven in the flowing bottom netting. The silver would lighten up the dreary day that no floodlights could illuminate. She briefly remembered the silver confetti from her promotion party. Ali shook herself.

"No need to go down a lonely road."

The dress was removed from the bag and the white plastic put on the top shelf of the closet with Lisa's baggage using up the rest of the space. The dress was lain out on the other queen size bed to keep wrinkles from developing. Ali previously unpacked her belongings into the home's bedroom drawers.

The designer of the dress couldn't make the shoot but sent her best regards with red roses and champagne. The hairstylist combed out the curls on the gorgeous brunette woman named Ali. The smoky eyeshadow was applied, the brows were enhanced, cheeks highlighted, and red lipstick with gloss was heavily applied. The model looked at herself in the mirror and could find no flaws with her image.

Ali walked out to the backyard near the wooded green pine trees. Their boughs were laden with snow. A hush surrounded the beautiful, picturesque setting. She walked the path the director showed her in a white fur coat.

The snow was fresh and soft. The snow machine would blow a few crystalline layers of snow around the bottom of her dress to hide her knee-high boots. Ali was glad she bought the fur lined leather boots to stand in the cold snow.

The director's helper told her the lighting was finally correct. They waited three days for a special meter to register the exact glow. During those three days, Ali skied the slopes with her boyfriend. She rarely saw Lisa. On the day of the shoot, Lisa finally appeared bubbling with excitement and bragging about the magazine company.

Now the moment had arrived, and Ali must perform to her best ability. For some reason, her excitement regarding the photo shoot was beginning to wear off. Lisa told her the problem was nerves. Ali wasn't sure. There was a feeling of dread. Ali couldn't shake the mood.

She handed back the fox coat and struck one of the poses the director requested. She repositioned herself too far. The cameraman motioned with his fingers the direction she should move. The cameraman took some photos and moved back and forth to catch the great images. The woods in the background would look slightly blurred in the pictures. Ali glanced at the woods when she heard something.

"I think there's a creature in the trees."

The cameraman looked through his lens.

"The trees are fine, Ali."

A cage was brought onto the set and placed on a table. Ali was confused. The director's helper took the black raven out of its cage and placed the bird on her bare arm. The bird's handler wasn't there but gave instructions to the helper.

An extra square piece of netting from her dress was draped over her flared sleeve to hide the bird's feet. The piece of netting touched Ali's bare skin.

"What is this? I never agreed to be photographed with a raven," complained Ali to the director.

The woman looked with disdain at the raven. The photographer took his best shots. The bird was the blackest of black and weighed two and a half pounds. The raven fluttered its large wings, uncomfortable with the woman's brutal stare. The raven kept staring and smelling her sweet perfume. The raven touched the red netting fascinated by the fabric. The fabric contained the woman's smell.

The director spoke, "Next pose, Ms. Zarin."

Ali turned sideways and looked directly into the raven's eyes. The camera clicked fast and many times. Ali wasn't sure why she was uncomfortable with the scene. She sneezed.

Great balls of snow fell from the trees and blew into her face.

"My hair and makeup are ruined."

The cameraman said, "Ali, you look great. Let's get a few more, please."

The camera clicked. Ali sneezed again. She was getting a cold. Her nose started to run. Suddenly, Ali picked up her dress, threw the bird and small square of fabric off her shoulder. She ran back to the house to get warm. The fur coat was left behind on the table with the raven cage in her rush to exit the scene.

"Well, I guess we are done for today. Everyone, let's disassemble and get out of here." The director only hoped there were a few good shots. He walked over to the cameraman who showed him the images.

"You're a genius. The images are a quality cover. Send them to the designer and the magazine per the model agency's request. Then we can all get paid. I'm going back to the lodge."

The director left the area with the fur coat to return the valuable item to a special rental company in Aspen. He left his crew to handle the cleanup or fall out in the area.

The bird was ripping a piece from the woman's fabric square. The bird was captured, put back in the cage, and taken back to the lodge lobby. The handler retrieved the raven and tried to take the netting from the bird. The raven squawked and pecked at his handler. The handler gave up and looked anxiously toward the door. He was ready to leave the lodge.

Back at the house, the designer's aide, Lisa Givens, helped the angry woman out of the red dress and left the bedroom.

Ali quickly got dressed in her white ski pants and sweater. She pulled her nylons off and put on wool ski socks. Scrambling to get her boots, she called the director of the modeling agency. He was still in Aspen.

"How dare you do this to me? Who paid for this ad? I talked with the designer on the phone today and she didn't know. This must be a joke. Someone in my past is playing tricks with me. I can't have those pictures published."

"Ali, please calm down. I'm sure there is a perfect explanation. I didn't know about the raven. The contract said there may be a pet. So, it's a bird. I understand he was tame, and the photos look great."

"I want to talk with you now. Meet me between the two slopes, Jupiter and Lower Mars, near the woods."

"Okay, I'll see you there. Let's hope they don't close the runs on us. We'll both be lucky to catch the last ski lift."

The director, Josh Jones, met her at the lift because she hadn't gone up yet. The operator didn't pay too much attention to the couple. They skied together to the edge of the woods and talked. Ali wouldn't back down from her request to withdraw the photos. He finally agreed to cancel the contract for her. The photographs would not be used. The director pushed off and skied down to the chalet.

Ali was still angry and wondered who set up this elaborate photo shoot with a raven. It was someone who knew her past intimately. If the pictures showed and her past was revealed, her career would be ruined. Her background wouldn't be appreciated by her viewers or her company.

She saw the path through the small wood. Ali waited for Lisa to arrive. They were friends and the designer aide would help sooth her spirits.

On a whim at Christmas, she purchased Lisa the same ski jacket, pants, and ski gear. The only difference were the ski goggles. Ali's goggle was black, and Lisa's was white.

The path through the woods was worn by other skiers. The path would take both women to the parking lot where they could get in Ali's vehicle. Ali was glad her boyfriend left earlier in the day for New York to visit friends. She would be alone to fix this mess before returning to work.

# RAIMENT RED AND A RAVEN

Halfway through the woods, a skier sped past the two women. His red one-piece ski suit and hat covered him fully. He wore dark ski goggles. The man stopped and waited for the two women to catch up to him. The women weren't alarmed. The ski patrols wore the same jacket and pant outfit.

Ali slowed and made a move to ski around him. Lisa was skiing faster and passed her. Suddenly the two women tripped on the wire and went down. The man rudely held out his pole which was pointed at Lisa's chest. He looked at Ali.

"Move or scream and I will kill her," said the man.

Ali motioned with her hands that she would comply. "What do you want?"

She looked up to see a gun with a silencer. The evil man smiled and without any hesitation, shot her friend point-blank in the forehead.

The blood splattered on the man who was standing. Ali's goggles also were sprayed with blood. Ali removed her goggles to see. The man took his goggles off and wiped them in the snow. Putting his gun away, he reached for his backpack and pulled out a knife.

Ali was unable to move away. Fear made her a statue of marble. The killer was delighted. With horrific speed, the skier plunged the knife into Ali's side. She groaned from the pain and shock, passing out, unconscious on the ground.

A white plastic dress bag was brought out. The bag was the same type that Ali's lavish red dress arrived in at the rental. He rolled the first dead woman's body inside, zipped the bag shut, and dragged her further into the woods. He kicked the first woman's ski poles out of the way towards her body. Then he dragged the other body off the trail. He regretted there wasn't a second white bag to hide his dirty deeds. The second set of ski equipment was placed over the second woman's head. The thrown snow was used to cover the second body.

The weatherman guessed correctly. A new batch of ice crystals were beginning to fall. There was no need to cover the blood on the ground. The man hurried out of the woods and skied to his car. With a sigh of relief, the killer noted the ski hill lights went out on the side runs of the mountain. No one would find the women for possibly a week.

Darkness settled over the ski valley. The wind slowed down around the tree line. *A hand moved in the damp, cold snow.*

One of the women was still alive. She touched her ski, gripping the metal and composite as if the ski was her lifeline. Her body froze when a tree branch snapped. Ali waited until she was sure the killer was no longer at the scene. Her cheeks were cold. It was time to move before she froze to death.

She saw the tracks in the snow and a hump. Using her hand, she found her ski poles and a branch. She snapped her skis in place and shoved off to the hump. Bending down was difficult. She dropped one ski pole beside the body. Ali managed to brush the snow away from the white plastic. Unzipping the bag, she saw Lisa's brunette hair spill out from her hood. Ali let out a sob. Moving her dead friend's head, she checked her pulse.

"Oh, Lis, I'm so sorry. This shouldn't have happened," said the woman softly to the darkness. She felt a piece of cloth stuffed in the hood by Lisa's face. The cloth appeared to be a handkerchief in size. Ali stuffed the cloth into her side pocket.

Fear enveloped Ali. The killer could come back. She needed to get away from the scene and figure out *why the killer was there in the woods at this lodge.* The *who* would come later. Somehow, she felt the cloth was possibly a clue.

She heard a raven's rasping call. The sound was familiar from when she lived near a Southwest Indian village in New Mexico. "There must be a raven's nest near."

Ali Zarin remembered long ago the last time she saw a common raven. The dead bird was placed in a tree and used to scare her. Someone stuffed the bird to make the thing look alive. Perhaps this bird call was an omen and its ancestors remembered her. She shouldn't have thrown the model raven away. The raven's black plumage lifted when she threw him into the air at the photo shoot, scaring everyone with her unkind movement.

"No, I shouldn't have brought Lisa on this late run with me. Lisa is dead because of my temper. Plus, there is my association with some bad person. What did I do to make this person so angry to want to kill me? Was it my success as an American news reporter? Was it the promotion?"

Ali would find out the answers. She would turn herself into the predator. She would let the raven's eyes guide her. The killer would become their prey.

Ali acknowledged her past. She moved as far away from the mean, hurtful teenager as possible. Her mother moved around the country for jobs when Ali was young. Ali was glad to leave the small town and a very disturbed young person. She even changed her name, hoping to remove that person's image from her mind and the bad memories. Yet, the now fully grown, crazy adult found her anyway. It was obvious that one of her questions was answered. Ali knew her possible attacker.

Rage fueled her body to find her dropped ski pole in the snow. Her side hurt. She could feel the blood seeping through the mesh and metal. The brace she wore for skiing protected her from the knife blow. The blade hadn't gone deep. There was a first aid case in her car. Her fanny pack was still around the waist and held her keys and identification.

She vowed to live to find Lisa's killer and finish off the threat to her life. To do that, she would need to disappear. Slowly, she descended the white, groomed hill on her skis to the bottom and freedom. There were no cameras on this side of the parking lot. Ali dropped her skis and gear in the trunk, started the engine, and slowly drove away. Her clothes were left at the lodge. She wouldn't need them anymore.

Driving down the road, she thought about the killer. "What if she was wrong about the person? Was there someone else just as demented and deadly?" Ali would need to move carefully to uncover the truth.

The reason for her hesitation was her newly-found success. Ali moved quickly up the corporate ladder. In her rise to a fantastic new job, she stepped on quite a few people. "No, I stepped on most of the people."

In her mind, Ali counted the list of people like a detective would do on a computer screen. Their faces and names were visible.

There was only one friend who might help her. Ali sighed. She wasn't sure her male friend would acquiesce to her style of detective work. She would need to convince him but not right now. First, she would need to assess the wound.

She brought her map out and selected the place to hide. The ranch was closer to Santa Fe, New Mexico. The ranch was where she saw her male friend the last time. Their parting was filled with hostility. He wanted Ali to leave her job in California and she refused. Now, here she would be, living in his house, where she refused to live before.

Thankful, the hacienda was far outside of town, she remembered the house contained over 4000 square feet with a secluded patio, and a four-stall garage. There was plenty of room and extra vehicles. Her friend's brother, Milan, lived on the property in another building as caretaker and handled the horses. The brother would not be surprised to see her and could be trusted. The brother could get her antibiotics.

There was a problem in that Milan would contact Grant. Grant Evans would be on the next plane

LINDA MCKOWN

from his fancy office in New York. Ali wasn't sure she could face Grant's anger again. Grant would feel forced to help her. His demeanor toward her would be one of aloofness. She could handle him. Too much time passed for there to be any sparks left.

Refocusing on the map and route, the distance would take more than seven hours. Stopping at a roadside diner, she assessed the line of vehicles in the back lot and began switching out her license plate.

She thought about Lisa and wondered when the authorities would find her body. Their checkout time from the lodge was in four days. There was plenty of time to formulate a new plan. It was too bad she would have to miss the funeral. Ali assumed the authorities would believe she was kidnaped. She, however, assumed wrong.

## 2 Month Before Attack

**CEO, Gene Fleming,** and news announcer, Ali Zarin, were in the conference room at the office. They spent many late nights together working the interview material for celebrities at the master's golf tournament.

"The material and contracts you've created were excellent. We've reviewed and edited the films. They've been released over the past several days while the tournament was playing. I know you've worked hard on all the minute details. Lisa Givens was supposed to help but called in sick. The ratings for the tournament were very high. The company is very pleased with our new Manager of the News. I'm promoting you, Ali, to the position. You know we have been looking for a couple months for the right fit. You're exactly our person. Congratulations!"

Ali made a move to get out of her chair. Her boss waved at her to sit down. Ali complied.

"My wife's input helped make the final decision about your new contract. She seems enamored with your skills and thought you would keep me out of trouble. She also knows that I want more free time to golf. Here is your new contract. We do appreciate your presence and the contract was written with you in mind. My wife and I want you to stick around for the next four years."

Ali read through the contract.

"Are you sure about the amount and meaning."

"Yes, we're sure. Two million dollars for the next four years, whether you perform your duties as manager or not is a fair contract. Many other executives make more than that amount. We left room for your salary to be re-negotiated after the first year."

Ali signed the new contract. The CEO said, "Now you can give me a hug."

Ali jumped up from her chair and hugged her boss. They waited for the woman from accounting to appear. Accounting gave Ali her copy of the contract and the rest was filed in company records. She put her contract in her briefcase. She would lock the briefcase in her desk before leaving. The next day she planned on going to the bank and would place the document in her lockbox.

"Thank you so much. I know there were other people in the company who also applied for the job. They are great news people. I hope they will be excited to work under me."

"I'm sure they are excited. The company has arranged a party at the country club after the tournament. I will make your promotion announcement there. Let's go to the party together. I've got the limousine ready. There's a massive bouquet of flowers for you with your name and title near the restaurant entrance. The food and drinks planned for this evening will be pricey. It's okay for us to take a break from work and cut loose. My wife will join us there."

The two people went to Ali's promotion party. The front buildings were reserved for their party. Any other country club guests were forced to use the hamburger bar and outside fireplace tables.

When they arrived, there was a massive crowd from the office waiting in the lobby for them. Congratulations and handshaking took a half and hour before the guests entered the restaurant area. The bar was busy for the rest of the evening.

Ali took a moment in the ladies' room to text her boyfriend. He was invited to the after-tournament party and had not yet arrived. She was concerned about his absence. She was so busy the last three weeks that they rarely saw each other.

One evening, Rad Newman complained to her about their relationship. He felt excluded from her life and wondered if they should break up. Ali assured him this was a once a year heavy commitment for her company that she must make happen.

If Rad was going to be on board for their relationship, he would have to get used to her work routine. Her job came first. The job would always be number one. Rad wasn't happy with her commitment to work. He started looking at other women.

Going back to the restaurant, she noticed Lisa Givens was missing from her co-workers.

The food trays came out and she sat down at the main table. The main table was highly decorated with more flowers and candles. Silver streamers with green ribbons were wrapped around the tables. Confetti was on the top white cloth. The main table contained the tournament team and their wives or escorts.

Ali was glad her chair was at the end. Her friend's empty chair wasn't quite so noticeable. The

CEO waived a photographer friend over to talk with him. Ali didn't know the chair was reserved for Lisa's spot.

The meal was escargot and bread or cold shrimp with tossed salad. Next came filet mignon or roasted chicken with baked potato or onion rings. The workers ate to their heart's content. No food scraps were left at the table. Extra coffee urns were deposited on the tables.

The CEO tapped his spoon against his coffee cup. The noise in the restaurant and bar died down.

"I am so glad some of you follow the gossip in our news room. Obviously, someone leaked my announcement of Ali's promotion because you all were way ahead of me. You were waiting at the door. I suppose I should blame the flower bouquet or accounting as they were the ones that wrote the twenty-five thousand dollar check to Ali Zarin for her hard work on the tournament. I know they didn't tell you her raise amount. Trust me, the amount is substantial. Let's show Ali our appreciation for her success."

The KMDZ-LA10 crowd cheered and whistled their approval.

"There also is another announcement. We have arranged a photo shoot in Aspen, Colorado, for Ali to pose as a model. She will possibly be on a magazine cover."

There was another round of cheers and Ali was surprised by the second announcement and wondered which magazine. She caught the word *possibly* but dismissed the word in her excitement.

"For the employees that were part of the tournament team, I've asked the mail room to put invitations in your mail slot. I've arranged a holiday as their bonus with five hundred dollars spending money. Each person will receive a three-day ski pass and lodge rooms in Aspen fully paid by the company at my favorite place. Accounting will coordinate your airplane tickets and car rentals. Again, those items will be courtesy of the company. We thank you for your help this year."

More cheering erupted across the country club. The large dessert cake was brought onto a table on the dance floor. The table meal dishes were put away to make room for the cake and ice cream.

The noise in the room increased in tone. Ali removed herself from the dessert area and walked to the end of their table. She read Lisa's nametag.

"Lisa missed dinner. Why?"

Ali finally saw Lisa who was moving toward the ladies' room. Ali turned to move in that direction when she ran into Rad. He was giving his coat to the coat check girl.

"Where have you been? I've been calling you most of the evening."

"Well, you can relax now. I'm here. I guess your hard work paid off. I'm going to the bar."

Ali was surprised by his abrupt departure. He didn't even congratulate her on her promotion. There was no explanation for his lateness such as traffic or an accident. Ali shook her head. Her boyfriend just gave her the brush off. She wasn't pleased.

She angrily pushed her way into the ladies' room. Lisa was combing her hair and swirling her pink lipstick case. She quickly ran the tube over her lips. Lisa dropped the items in her purse and turned.

"Ali, congratulations." Lisa said sweetly and hugged Ali. Lisa appeared delighted about her promotion.

"You missed dinner?"

"I couldn't get here in time. I'm always running late. I saw the photographer talking to the boss. I didn't want to interrupt."

"I know you applied for the job, too. Mr. Fleming told me the names of the other candidates."

"I'm surprised he shared the candidate information with you. My, my, you've arrived at the trusted upper crust of the company. How lovely?"

"Lisa, I'm sorry we couldn't both be in the trust circle."

"Yes, I did apply. But I can wait for my shot at fame. Don't worry about me. I have plans. I did hear the CEO told everyone about Aspen. You must be thrilled. Now you and Rad can go skiing."

Ali thought of Rad at the bar. He didn't even wear a tie and his suit was wrinkled. She still wondered why he was late.

"I haven't asked him yet. He seemed a little off when I saw him arrive. Sometimes he is up and then he is down. I wonder if he's taking pills or weed."

"I wouldn't worry about him. He's dispensable. You and I know men. Here today, gone tomorrow. They like to look and touch. But Rad Newman can be fun when he wants and loves to ski. Taking a break will be good for you. I'm sure he will be delighted to go on the trip. You really need to ask him."

Lisa left the ladies room.

Ali looked at her image in the mirror. Her hair was fine. Her black business suit and white silk blouse was beautiful. The CEO pinned a rose corsage to her lapel earlier. Her face was flushed and happy despite Rad.

"Girl, you're high on your own success."

One of the girls from accounting walked by her.

"Way to go, Ali, talking to yourself already. I understand this happens when a person is surprised. You were my female pic for making the top. Usually the company selects the men for the high positions. Us women need to stick together. Don't tell anyone I said those words. Equal opportunity for all is the company motto. Nice contract by the way. Not to worry, my lips are sealed or else I'm gone, and I like my job just fine."

Ali laughed, thanked the woman, and smiled. Her mood was lightened by the thought of her new contract. She already took over many new responsibilities from the CEO. The work ahead at the news company would be familiar.

It was time to mingle with her co-workers and talk to Rad. She went to the bar and ordered herself a glass of white wine. Rad had several empty glasses in front of him.

"You're having fun."

"I always have fun, beautiful."

Ali was pleased Rad calmed down.

"Would you like to fly with me and go skiing for three days?"

"Now you ask me. Let me check my calendar."

Ali took a sip from her wine and tried to get off the bar stool.

Rad stopped her.

"I'll go. We should have a good time skiing. I checked the weather report. I was stalling. My calendar is free."

Ali sat down. Somehow, she didn't think they would have a good time in Aspen. It was too late to retract the vacation invite.

Ali would make sure he was put in a separate room at the lodge. Co-workers liked to talk. Now that she was manager, she needed to be careful of her image. Ali thought the room would be one more reason for her boyfriend to be upset with her. Arrangements were made for Ali and Lisa to stay in a rented home.

There was distance between her and Rad that needed repair. He acted strange and aloof lately. She wondered how she was going to repair the damage. Ali needed to ask herself serious questions. Ali wasn't sure she needed Rad in her life now that she was on her way to bigger venues.

Unknown to Ali, there were people moving around her like a pack of wolves. Each wolf was waiting for the opportune moment to attack. The booty was high. She would be caught in the middle.

# RAIMENT RED AND A RAVEN

There would be few places to hide. Fate would force the woman to turn to someone in her past. Her life would be in danger of invasion by killers. It would be difficult to decide who was her real friends.

Ali went home alone after the party. She called a taxi. Taking her business suit off, there were a few silver pieces of confetti in her pocket. She let them fall to the floor. Emptiness filled her heart and she softly sobbed. She didn't know what was wrong with her. This should have been a very happy day.

"I must be coming down with a cold. That's why I'm shaking and lonely."

## 3 Skiing in Aspen

**Rad and Ali** let their bodies slip into sitting position as the ski lift chair came around. The ski lift operator was friendly and talked to the guests as the chair slowed so they could get on. The chair lifted them higher to the black runs which is where they would ski for four hours. They took a break midway at one of the upper ski lodges, eating hot dogs and French fries. Ali drank ginger water and Rad drank a cola.

"Now that was fun. It's been some time since we went skiing. I like my body remembering how to bend at the appropriate time."

"I'm glad you could keep up with me on the moguls. Your working out at the gym has helped, Ali."

Rad seemed in good spirits and Ali enjoyed the rigor of skiing down the runs. Their first day was enjoyable together. They flew over the mogul runs and competitively raced each other to the middle lift.

Ali began to relax and feel comfortable in their relationship when Rad fell and lost a buckle on his ski boot. Ali slowly accompanied him to the main lodge at the bottom of the hill.

"I'm done for the day. I'll see if the ski shop can help me. The lost and found might have the old one. I do have a new buckle in my suitcase. The ski shop may be able to attach the new one or steer me to a local company in town."

"All right. I'll catch the bus back to the house rental and meet with you for dinner."

Rad called Ali to let her know he was still at the repair shop and wouldn't be able to meet her for dinner. He would see her tomorrow for skiing.

Ali ordered a pizza and salad delivered to the rental for herself. Lisa was meeting with friends at the lodge and wouldn't be back until after midnight.

"Well, this is not how I planned my vacation, sitting alone. Hopefully, tomorrow will be better."

There were only four more hours of skiing and Rad twisted his ankle on an easy blue run. A ski patrol stopped, and they pulled Rad down the hill on a stretcher with a snowmobile. Ali followed and waited for their recommendation. An ambulance was called, and the doctor took some x-rays. There were no broken bones. Rad only sprained his leg and should rest easy for the next week.

Lisa arrived at the hospital overly concerned about his ability to walk. Ali drove them back to the lodge. Rad decided he couldn't do dinner again and Lisa went off to buy takeout Chinese for him. On the way back from the restaurant she dropped Ali at the rental. Lisa would need the car for the evening to meet some new friends after depositing Rad's takeout containers. Ali loaned a new stretch black dress to Lisa for dancing.

Ali was alone for dinner the second night. She thought about contacting some of her co-workers at KMDZ-LA10 about seven o'clock. By then, her friends left their rooms for dancing in town.

28

Sitting on her bed, Ali stared at the red gown. Lisa decided to sleep on the rental's couch. She explained there was no reason to disturb Ali's sleep.

"Lisa's having more fun than I am. I really liked my black dress. I don't know what possessed me to let her wear my dress. My wearing the item in the future won't be the same. The dress will feel slightly damaged."

Ali sighed, "I can always take the dress to the secondhand store."

Ali touched the red gown. She knew the dress was on loan from the designer. She wouldn't need to wear the red dress again.

"At least I won't need to ski with Rad anymore. This is one of the worst vacations of my life."

Ali went over to her luggage and opened her case. There was an old airline ticket to Albuquerque in the pocket.

She remembered her other vacation with Grant Evans.

"At least, Grant, you didn't disappear in the evenings. We always ate a nice dinner before we argued."

Ali began to think about Rad. His disappearances were too much. She wondered if he faked his fall. The leg didn't look highly swollen. She wondered what he would say if she dropped by his room. Then she thought better of it.

"Let sleeping dogs lie."

Instead she made an airplane out of her old ticket and flew the paper into her mirror where the item crashed.

"There goes another relationship down the hill."

She didn't want to lean on Rad any more. Their relationship was deader than the airplane. Ali crumpled the ticket and angrily threw the item in the trash.

Next, she took the ticket out of the trash and smoothed the ticket. She was remembering a horse ride with Grant, a barbeque, a kiss, and much more.

"Familiarity staves off loneliness."

Ali almost called Grant on his line in New York. She stopped herself. Her future with the news company changed. Her career was the bright star she would hang her dreams.

"Men, right now, were a slippery and rocky slope."

Eventually she would need to inform Rad about her feelings. At least they didn't purchase a condominium together in New York. He pressured her about owning property together. She resisted and felt fortunate to have avoided further entanglement. Lawyers were expensive. Even a friend who was a lawyer would be high priced. Ali thought it funny if she hired Grant Evans as her lawyer. She stopped laughing.

"Grant would refuse to be her lawyer under those circumstances. Girl, time to go to bed. You're thinking like a nut-case."

Ali went to the rental window and looked outside toward the tree line before she pulled the drapes closed. A man outside watched her.

## 4 Newspaper Headlines

Once the body of Lisa Givens was found, the police cordoned off the entire ski lift, ski run, woods, and parking lot.

The stone-cold body was silently taken away in a black hearse. The snow melted in the spot where her body was found. No sirens heralded her death. Quiet comes quickly for those unprepared.

The lodge again bustled with activity the next day. The place became the location for all types of police and detectives. Guests canceled their reservations to stay as far away from the area as possible.

The restaurants were empty, and the food remained in the freezers. The bread delivery was canceled. The lodge owners were busy trying to rebook the skiers for a later visit to their mountain.

The sudden warm weather after the storm was a disaster for their business. The murder added the final drop in business. No amount of PR was going to fix the owner's problem. The owner's hope was for the police to exit the area. He hired a lawyer for help.

Detective Candace Moon walked around the scene with her new partner, Doug Constantine.

"What happened to Mackenzie? She was supposed to be here to investigate the crime."

"I don't know. Your boss called me. He thought this one required a different kind of mind. He told me my last investigation was a gut-wrench of a job. Your boss liked my stamina until the case closed."

"Your mind is better than Mackenzie. No way. She does hate snow and probably begged off the case. We need to stop wasting time and take a hard look."

Her skis crunched in the snow. She removed her skis as did Doug. He rubbed his knees and looked at the tree line area. Candace moved closer to the space indicated by the police map and tape.

"This crime scene is an absolute mess. Per the coroner, our victim has been dead five days. Five freaking days for thousands of skiers to wander over this area. We don't know what pieces belong to the death scene, and what pieces don't. The killer found enough time to fly to Canada with the geese and come back twice."

Doug assessed the woods, "I like Canada. Been there once. Vancouver, I think. I didn't see any geese."

Candace threw a snow ball at him.

"Hey, that's not fair."

"Are you in Canada or at this investigation?"

Doug moved closer. "This place looks like a herd of cattle came through chased by a pack of ravenous wolves from Alaska."

"I think you mean coyotes. I believe Colorado has coyotes or else it's Arizona."

"Gray wolves might have migrated from Wyoming. Look, whatever and wherever our animals came from is fine. I agree we have a mess."

Detective Moon groaned, "Mackenzie, I'm going to kill you for slipping out and leaving me with a new detective who talks in riddles."

# LINDA MCKOWN

She was also talking in riddles. The two detectives saw the dead body and pictures of Lisa Givens. Now they were at the crime scene. The riddles and bantering were a protection mechanism to deflect the horror they witnessed about the murder of a young woman. Candace wanted to walk away and go home. She forgot her problem and concentrated on her keen skills. She was important to the discovery of the truth. The family trusted her skills. Her boss did the same.

Doug scratched his head and looked at the outline of where the dead woman lay and the distance to the trail.

"Obviously, she was shot in the forehead on the trail after tripping on a wire. There was no time for her to scream for help. She was dead instantly and the killer staged the body off the trail. We saw the white dress bag. The bag might have been from Ali's room. He left the ski gear. The killer then, probably skied down to the parking lot to make his getaway."

Candace looked blankly at Doug in his mismatch ski jacket and khaki slacks. His acrylic hat read *bottoms up*. Obviously, he wasn't a true skier. She remembered he told her about ice skating as a kid.

Candace laughed. Doug more than likely did the snowplow all the way down the hill to the death scene. She would have loved to see him do the snowplow. Now, Candace wished she could be back at the lodge with a cup of chocolate. She always thought better holding something warm.

"What's so funny?" Doug just wanted to wrap up this disconcerting meeting at the crime scene and get someplace warmer like LA.

Candace noticed there wasn't any snow on Doug's rear. He wisely didn't fall on his way to the scene.

"Do you think that I didn't already get those pieces of information, Sherlock? There is just something about this mess that is wrong. Per the lift operator, he thought two women and a man were on the last ride up the hill. The lift operator identified the three people. One woman is dead, and the director is alive. So, where is the second woman? They must have been together. Ali Zarin and Lisa Givens never checked out of the lodge. Both women's clothing and suitcases are still there. We checked with Ms. Zarin's boyfriend. He didn't do the dirty kill because he was delayed on his return in an airport far away from the crime. Ali, his girlfriend, is missing. This was supposed to be a holiday vacation and a little side job modeling for Ali.

"The lodge and resort are a nice vacation spot. Too bad things ended differently for one of the guests," said Doug.

Candace looked around the wooded spot.

"Correction, two of the guests. Did Ali run from the murderer? I would have, except the killer held a gun. Our guess is there was a silencer so as not to trigger an avalanche. If she got away, how could she have done that with a killer near? Freaking miracle maybe. If we're into a miracle, why hasn't she come forward? If she's dead, where's the blood? Where is she? Too many ifs. I feel like I'm in Algebra class."

Doug knew she was not going to like the word, "Kidnapping?"

Candace paced back and forth. "I don't think that happened. We found her cell phone in the parking lot broken into bits. There was probably a tire wheel that crushed the phone, except her car is missing. A witness saw two cars in the lot. The witness didn't think two cars were unusual. The killer would have also had a car. How could he drive two cars away from the area? He couldn't and didn't. Therefore, no kidnaping."

"Well, at least we can begin questioning the director and other persons involved in the photo shoot."

Candace said, "I already phoned them last night and checked out the consulting agency who coordinated the setup. They were the company that hired the shoot. The magazine company knew nothing about the bogus cover. They were insulted when the police stopped by their office. No one will be happy when they find out they aren't getting paid a dime for their time and expenses. Unless they were paid in full upfront. The next question would be by whom?"

"Crap, the by whom means more work for me?"

"Sherlock, I need you to travel to Los Angeles and talk with people who worked with and for Ali and Lisa. I'll go chase down Ali and Lisa's parents to see if there is some piece of information they can provide."

Doug looked at Candace. "I will on one condition. I know that I'm new to your style of investigating. I have my own way to uncover the truth.

We both want to catch the perp. Stop calling me Sherlock."

"Okay, big boy. Go do your detective stuff." Candace turned her skis around. She stopped.

"The trees where the wire was placed, we need to check them."

Doug turned back to the trees marked with a white "*X*" by the police.

"Why do they always use the letter?"

"Here marks the spot takes too long."

"You're funny, Detective Moon."

"The assumption was the women were skiing together and hit the wire. We see the area where they searched. Let's think about the skiing. Perhaps Ali slowed down. Instead of landing far out, she lands closer to the trees. We know the weather. There was snow. This area is filled with snow. No ski tracks. Why don't we do squares with our ski poles?"

"Good idea." Doug picked the first row of squares and Candace moved eighteen inches outward in the next row. They alternated. Doug faked his ski pole touching something. He dug a piece of gum out of his pocket and rolled the yellow wrapper into a ball.

"Oh, look a gold nugget."

Candace was miffed.

"Give me that. Gold wouldn't be this high up. There's no creek either. A piece of gum, really."

Doug slipped and slid like he was on a piece of ice.

"Very funny. Now you're messing up the grid."

"No, I made sure to dance in an already checked spot."

Doug felt something hit his boot.

"There's a piece of wood. The object is probably a stick. No, the object is plastic."

Detective Moon ignored Constantine.

He pulled out black ski goggles. She looked up. Doug's goggles were on his hat.

"Oh, my. The goggles in the snow are real."

There appeared to be dried blood on the inside and possibly on the band.

Candace hurried to the spot and took pictures. They bagged the goggles. They saw a larger broken branch.

"She probably passed out. When she came to, she leaned on the branch for support to get back up. I don't see any blood on the branch. There'd be no fingerprints if she left her gloves on. The tracks in the snow the killer made would be fresh. Ali sees the tracks. She skis over to what appears to be her friend and realizes she is dead."

"Or we already know who our killer might be, and they accidentally dropped their goggles," said Doug.

Doug couldn't see Candace's face. He figured he said the wrong thing again. He kept quiet.

"I don't think Ali would kill her friend. There were too many witnesses who saw them on the ski lift. Where's her motive? The news woman was well known. She recently received a promotion and we'll assume raise. No motive clicks off again in my brain. We must return to the lodge, inform our boss, and get the goggle sent to the lab. The police shouldn't have missed the item."

"There's a reason for detectives. Our minds are more creative." Doug put on his skis.

Candace slowly skied with him back to the lodge. They were pleased with the new evidence. The past evidence collected at the scene were Lisa's broken ski goggles, gear, wire, the white dress bag, and body.

There was additional reason to keep the area closed after three weeks of combing the area. The pressure from her peers was there to allow the lodge to restart the ski run. There would be further delay.

Permission was given to the parents to cremate the body of their daughter and have a funeral. Meanwhile, life went around and around.

Candace returned her ski rental equipment and sat in her vehicle in her navy-blue ski outfit drinking hot chocolate. Her white hat and gloves were removed.

"Don't worry. We'll catch you. Crime never pays is my motto. I don't know which one of you killed Lisa, male or female. One of you is on the run. Or one of you isn't scared at all and is in plain view. Which type of crazy am I chasing? But then, you don't know me. You're one person that needs to be locked away. Be aware, I'm not scared either. The past gives me clues."

Candace didn't tell Doug the mother of Lisa revealed a strange man approached her daughter a couple months ago about Ali. The strange man gave Lisa a card. He wanted Lisa to have Ali call him. He said they were old friends. Lisa left the card on her mom's dresser. The mother assumed that her daughter never gave the information to Ali. The card was from a man named, Latin Dooley, taxidermist in Nevada. Taxidermist meant a stuffer of dead animals. The word *unusual* came to Candace's quiet thoughts.

She would need to give the information to Doug. Eventually, they would visit the man together. Candace checked out Dooley's website and chat information. His pictures showed rooms of stuffed animals. There were no pictures of a wife or family.

"Definitely, stranger danger. I do need Sherlock on this visit."

Looking at the two photos of Lisa and Ali, Candace noticed how similar their features were. Their height and weight were close on their driver's license. They worked in the same office. "Competition for the same job? Ali already won the job."

She looked at the crime scene photos on her cell phone. The white ski jacket with blood had once been beautiful like the victim. There was real fur on the hood and the label looked expensive. The whole ski outfit and gear cost bucks. She made a mental note to see how many sizes 8 white jackets by this brand were sold and to whom.

"Mistaken identity? Naw. Lisa's mom told us the two women were workplace friends."

Another photo appeared in her view. "The red dress on the bed was beautiful for a cover magazine. The raven at the photo shoot seemed an outdated idea. She read the glamour magazines. Most places photoshopped the tigers and leopards in their ads.

Gothic photo? The raven belonged in a historical novel."

She looked at the open door of the rental home's bedroom closet. She saw Lisa's red luggage with pink tags. Ali's one bag and briefcase were black. Her clothes were in the next picture, neatly folded in the drawers. Most of her clothes were black or white.

"Both women were super neat. Neat meant an organized mind. Or at least a detail-oriented one. Then she saw the bathroom with Lisa's messy makeup. The items were emptied on the counter and the bag with the *L* was thrown aside. One was a little messy."

Candace shifted in the car seat.

"Ali's goggles were black. The raven was black. Death is black. Some people believe the raven is a bad omen. The raven is a friend or enemy. Friends or enemies? Which one was the prey? Ali Zarin, you may be in trouble. Or you committed the crime and are my killer?"

Candace saw her boss walking over to her rental vehicle to discuss the situation. He wouldn't be happy either when she told him they obtained few clues to the Lisa Givens murder case and disappearance of an up-and-coming news woman. She would keep her ideas to herself about Ali Zarin.

The paper cup was thrown out the window into the nearest trash bin. She missed and would need to get out of the car to pick the darn cup up. The effort would be another part of a long day for her. She thought again about the killer. The list of possibilities for suspects was increasing.

Candace needed more time and more detective work. She thought about her new partner, Doug. She informed her boss the new man might work. Her boss wanted Doug's expertise. Candace locked the rental car and went inside the lodge.

"Let's hope Ali is not a killer.

## 5 Hacienda Hideaway

**Ali turned left** on the familiar dirt road which was a quarter mile from the buildings. The drive to the ranch took her longer than expected. She stopped at a motel and drugstore. She fought a fever for three days before she could continue driving.

The wrought iron sign read the name, *Evans Ranch*. The second gate contained the cattle gate and a *No Trespassing* sign. A large curved cement structure shielded the driveway from the main road. She parked her vehicle and went to the doorbell.

Before she could press the bell, the heavy wooden door opened, and Milan hugged her.

"We thought you were kidnapped or dead. Here you are. Everyone is looking for you. Come in. I'll move your car inside the garage. There is a reason you came here. Not to worry, my brother and I will keep you safe."

"Thank you, Milan, but I need to rest a minute. Do you have any antibiotics?" She pulled up her sweater that was still stained with her blood to show him the leaking bandage.

Milan grabbed a bottle of pills from his bathroom and threw her a bottle of water.

"I'll be back to help you clean, change bandage, and put on new clothes. You left clothes in your room last time you were here."

Ali took some medication and went to her bedroom. The pills would halt the infection. She dropped her fanny pack on the bed and hung her coat on the chair. Opening a few drawers, she selected a new flannel shirt, slacks, and underwear. There was no need for a bra to rub on her wounds.

Milan came back and knocked on her door. He handed the bandage packet, wound cleaner, antiseptic, tape, and scissors through the door crack.

"I can help you with your bandage."

Ali laughed, "No, thanks and no peeking."

"A man can always try to help a lady. I'll make us some sandwiches and we can talk. It's a good thing we have no visitors today. I will need to feed the horses as my hired hand is away for three weeks. His mother passed away and he flew to Mexico for the funeral."

"Fine, I'm starving now that you mentioned food. I'll be about ten minutes. Oh, please don't call Grant. I have my reasons."

"All right. You know that I don't like to keep anything from him. I owe him my life for giving me a chance to work here. He would want to know that you are safe."

"I do know and I'm sorry. I will explain later," said Ali.

The final piece of tape was applied. She threw her sweater in the trash and tried to wash the blood out of her jacket. She gave up and brought both items out to the laundry room. Adding a large dose of soap and cool water, Ali placed the items in the large laundry tub. The fur was removed from the collar.

Walking out to the kitchen, she sat down at the bar stool. The telephone land line rang, and the recorder picked up the message. Ali listened to the woman named Alessandria leave a sympathetic message for Grant about his missing friend, Ali."

"The designer, she's sorry, my ass. The call is a cheap shot at best for his sympathy or a way to offer more of her services."

Ali wanted to delete the message and thought better of it. She looked out the living room window.

"I love this view. We are up high in the mountain, and you can see for miles."

Ali went back to the bedroom to see how many clothes were in the drawers. Milan came into the kitchen, listened to the phone message, and quickly deleted the call. He hoped Ali hadn't heard Alessandria.

Coming back into the kitchen, Ali sat down on a bar stool. Her face was unreadable.

Milan was pleased to have someone to talk with at the ranch. "We should eat and talk with coffee."

Milan handed her a stoneware mug and the two friends ate in silence. He turned the music on softly, hoping the sound would bring back fond memories of her time visiting the ranch.

Reluctantly she went to the L-shaped couch and sat down with pillows propping her feet.

"You've seen the news, I'm sure."

Milan nodded. "Hold just a second, I forgot the sugar cinnamon." He came back and handed her the bowl. Ali stirred the sweet stuff. Sugar helped put a person in a good mood.

"My friend and co-worker, Lisa Givens, was murdered with a gun by a killer. There was no time to save her. I was stunned. The lodge was our favorite place for skiing. My boyfriend came to ski. Lisa and I went back to the ski hill after a photo shoot. We shouldn't have been in the trees. The killer decided to use a knife on me. I was fortunate."

Milan remembered when they went skiing together on a vacation in Lake Tahoe.

"Your brace. You wore your brace and the knife deflected. The killer wasn't careful and left you alive. I understand that now you are in danger. The killer must know you are alive, especially with no body at the death scene. He will be looking for you. We'll protect you. We have an arsenal of guns and cameras here. Also, there are lots of Grant's friends we can trust."

"Why did you say the killer was a man?"

"Men use guns and knives. Also, they use trip wires. Women don't like wires. They might use a cliff to shove someone off instead. I've dated a few women who wanted to kick my butt into the next county. They would think the cliff was a short cut."

Ali couldn't help but smile. Milan's affairs with women were usually a disaster.

Milan continued. "I've been riveted to the news channels since we heard you were missing. Now that you are here, it is important for you to heal while my brother and I think up a plan. There is an enemy out there who will track you. Your enemy's heart is hard and black as an onyx stone. His plan for you would be bad."

Ali drank the wonderful Mexican bean coffee with just the right amount of sugar cinnamon.

"I need time to heal and think. Whatever plan is formulated, I want into the game. This person tried to kill me and did kill a friend. Black evil personified is correct in describing the attacker. His heart is a piece of stone."

Milan brought the coffee and refilled her cup.

"I have to warn you that some of the news media are being unkind. They will believe the worst. You do not have to defend yourself to us. We know who you are, and we love you."

"Thank you, but what do you mean by unkind."

Milan wished his older brother was here.

"The news media are hinting that you might be the killer of Lisa, and that is why you disappeared."

Ali was shocked. Her running away didn't solve anything.

"That is totally absurd. I have no reason to hurt Lisa. I bought her the ski outfit, gear, and invited her to stay with me in Aspen. She was a friend. We've known each other a long time. I know after my promotion, she avoided me. There were no deskside chats after the news show. I tried to talk with her. Next thing I knew, she was out of the office for a week. When she came back, Lisa was all bright and cheery. We were fine together."

"Still, I think we need Grant's expertise here. He's a better thinker and tracker than I am. He'll know how to proceed. You need to make a list of possible people who aren't friendly. Lisa and any of her co-workers should be included. Something is up. Unless we have a random killer roaming the ski slopes which I find unlikely. Usually, there's too many people and too few means of escape. Now a large city is a perfect spot for killers to roam. No offense about your living in LA. With your list Grant will check everyone thoroughly."

"I've thought about the unusualness of the attack. My mind is having a hard time wrapping around the scene."

Ali went into her bathroom and brought back the handkerchief that she found on Lisa at the crime scene.

"The killer left this handkerchief, stuffed into Lisa's hood. The handkerchief is mine."

"How did your handkerchief get there? Did you use it to wipe away Lisa's blood?"

"No. The handkerchief was a message. The killer made a mistake by leaving it. A long time ago, a teenager tricked me by leaving me with a dead raven in the woods. I was scared at first, but realized the bird was stuffed and couldn't hurt me. I used my handkerchief with the pink flowers to hold the bird while I untied him. Then I set the bird in the crook of the tree so that in death, it could fly. I know that sounds silly, but we lived around a group of Southwest Indians for a while. They always told me stories."

Milan understood. "The photo shoot with the raven was fake. You were set up by someone who wanted to scare you again. There is someone from your past playing dangerously close. Interesting. You might know who the killer is."

"Yes, I believe I do. The raven scare was a long time ago. Why would the man wait this long to come after me? Unless there are other people involved. Nothing makes any sense."

Milan nodded. This murder was taking on a whole different perspective. Seeing, Ali yawn a couple times, he suggested they retire until morning. Ali was more than ready to crawl into a soft bed with fluffy coverlet and nice pillows. The ranch was built with comfort in mind. She took some aspirin and was fast asleep.

Milan fed and watered the horses. He checked the few cows earlier in the day. They were fine until morning. Slowly, he went into his brother's den and made the call. He would sleep in the house tonight until his brother arrived the next day. He brought out three of the hand guns and placed them around the house in the spots his brother designated. They would be ready in case any intruders came. Milan didn't believe anyone knew Ali was at their ranch.

Grant told him, "You can never be sure who's prowling around. We should be prepared for anything. Ali's company knew we once dated. My ranch is a possible area of interest to the media, police, and killer."

Milan remembered the phone call from Alessandria and gave Grant the message.

Grant groaned.

"Alessandria left me a message in New York. I haven't called her back. She wanted to meet for dinner. I have no plans to see her nor require any future design advice. I'd better do the call right away. Otherwise, she will visit the ranch. I don't want Alessandria to know about my arrival. Her suspicious nature could be a problem."

The two brothers hung up. Milan grabbed a magazine and took the first watch. He was glad his older brother was coming. He knew Ali would be upset but she always calmed down.

"She belongs here. The ranch was her home as far as Milan was concerned. Ali always came home."

Grant caught the last flight to Albuquerque. He would stay the night with a friend who would drive him to the ranch early in the morning. He told Milan to say nothing. He didn't want Ali to bolt. Grant watched all the latest developments on the news. He knew the trouble they were all facing. Hiding a suspected criminal was a problem, but necessary.

"Innocent until proven guilty sometimes works. Ali, what have you gotten yourself into this time? Or has some SOB been waiting all this time for payback? Maybe this person is someone newer? We've been out of touch so anything or anyone could be playing havoc with your life. I will have lots of questions when we meet. I hope you are prepared," said Grant.

## 6 Reckoning with Grant

**She awoke at** four in the morning with her side hurting. The bandage was soaked. Ali looked at her ashen face in the mirror. Her silk nightshirt would need to be removed and placed in cold water much like her sweater and jacket.

The nightmare and cold woke her. She could feel the freezing cold snow underneath her in the dream. All she could remember was the sound the silencer made and laying on the ground with blood. In her nightmare dream, she tried to scream but couldn't.

Ali remembered a drawer in her room and went to pull the white T-shirt from its confines. She smelled the fragrant cologne that belonged to Grant. Memories engulfed her. The shirt was stuffed there a long time ago when his father was still alive. Grant sneaked into her room on her first visit and they spent the night.

Taking the shirt into the bathroom, she redid her bandage and pulled the soft cotton over her head. The silk pajamas were placed in the sink with bath soap and water. Ali crawled back in bed and pulled the warmth to her almost bare frame. She was out for the rest of the early morning.

Grant arrived, talked briefly with his brother, and went to Ali's room. He stayed there in a chair until she stirred. Daylight was filtering into the room as she awakened. She saw him in a haze and reached out. He took her hand and warmed it with his breath. Ali felt cold. Suddenly, she was fully awake.

"Grant, you shouldn't be here."

"You do know this is my ranch."

Ali frowned and suddenly remembered there were no underpants. She couldn't exactly escape to the bathroom. He saw her alarm.

"Don't worry, I already noticed when I lifted your shirt and the bandage to check your wound. The knife cut looks long and nasty. But I believe you will live. And by-the-way, you do look good without underwear. Where did you find the shirt?"

"Stuffed in the drawer."

"Ah, yes, I do remember that first night."

Ali blushed. She didn't know what to say.

"You could tell me how glad you are, Ali, to see me. It's been quite some time."

"I heard you were seeing a gallery designer."

"You heard correctly. She was helping me buy Southwestern pottery, specifically orange and white in color."

"I heard there was more to your relationship."

Grant wondered if that was why she stayed away. He needed to correct the gossip mill.

"She wanted more but I wasn't interested. We did go to dinner several times. There never was anything beyond dinner."

"There was a picture in a magazine of you kissing Alessandria Morgan."

Grant sighed. He didn't want to talk about Alessandria.

"She is a beautiful woman and I do like to kiss one on occasion. You've also kissed the opposite sex lately."

Ali was silent contemplating his words. She looked toward the window noting that the drapes were pulled tightly shut.

Grant could see she was shutting him out. He was aware of the signs.

"Okay, it's too early for talking. Why don't I let you get dressed while I make us some good old-fashioned hash browns, bacon, and eggs for breakfast. Then we can talk about this problem of yours."

Grant left her alone with her thoughts and her feelings. Ali thought about the back door and her vehicle in the garage. She could run. "Run to where?"

Reluctantly she took a sponge bath, dressed, and went to the kitchen where the smells were delicious.

He was glad to see her in a soft blue velour jogging suit and peach-checked wool socks. She tied her hair into a ponytail with a peach hair tie.

Grant left Ali's clothes and makeup in the bedroom in the hopes she would come back at least to retrieve them. He was glad the clothes were in the drawers. They wouldn't need to order her new items.

He flipped the switch to the kitchen gas fireplace. The fireplace fake logs instantly came alive. The kitchen warmed. This was the only fireplace on the place that didn't burn wood.

"Thank you. I've been very cold. My body is probably fighting the effects of shock and the stabbing."

Grant plunked down the handmade earthenware plate filled with everything including toast and fruit. He poured her fresh-squeezed orange juice and a cup of coffee. Sitting down next to her, he placed a napkin in her lap gently squeezing her knee.

"You're more than likely right. Let's eat my love."

Ali noted his slip in words. He hadn't called her that name in a long time. She looked at him in alarm. He was oblivious and was devouring the breakfast meal.

"I noticed the mesquite trees planted to the east of the house. The trees add wonderful texture to the landscape. The wood will come in handy for barbeques. I've found this wonderful cookbook about New Mexico barbeques. There's a picture of a whole hog on a pit. You'd like the sauces."

Grant shook his head. "Ali, stop being sociable. We aren't on your news program and I'm not in the mood. We're going to sit down and talk so you better eat breakfast. The bacon is from a friend who likes black pepper."

Ali hated it when he bossed her around. However, she was exhausted from tossing and turning all night. Things needed to be settled between them if she was going to receive his help.

"The bacon's good."

Ali didn't want to stop talking about simple food. She resented Grant pushing her away from normalcy.

Grant felt guilty for bossing her. She made him angry. She was still beautiful, and he still wanted her. He was thinking about his job in New York. Maybe it was time for him to move back home. He left the area when she refused to stay. Now he was rethinking his motives.

Grant was a former sheriff in the area. His father talked him into going to law school. He became a good lawyer with a firm in New York. Now he made a lot of money. There was enough to keep a penthouse in the city and keep his beloved ranch. He knew the slime that existed in the world. He saw both sides every day.

Someone tried to kill a very wonderful, close friend. He was angry at more than Ali. He hated the person who killed her friend and was able to get close enough to damage Ali's skin. The knife wound would have finished her without the brace. Her pain was his pain. It would always be this way for him.

He looked over and saw Ali was silent. She did eat her breakfast and was full of a warm meal. Grant stepped over to remove her plate. Their fingers accidentally touched. He couldn't stop the forward motion. Grant walked around the bar and gently took her into his arms. He let Ali weep and helped her wipe the tears away with the cloth napkin.

"I still love you and I'm sorry you are hurting. I'll do everything I can to help whether you want me or not."

Ali turned her face to him and kissed him full on the lips.

"Thank you one more time for being my friend. I really appreciate your kindness. Now I'm ready and we can talk."

Grant gently led her to the couch where her story unfolded. He knew her disclosure was the beginning of getting well. There was no one else she could talk to right now. He was glad that he returned to the hacienda. She didn't know yet there was more than help that he was willing to offer her. A raven flew over to the mesquite trees.

Grant saw the raven. The raven was following Ali. This was a good sign. The bird was tenacious. He would be, too.

He kept the blue velvet box in his drawer. The box held a platinum pear-shaped diamond ring. Grant never returned the item to the jewelry store. The jewelry store owner later sent the wedding band when Grant requested the item. This was after he completed the cabin in the pinyons.

He planned on contacting Ali in the future. Life and death got in the way. This was not the time or place to talk with Ali about their future. Fate pushed her back into his arms. This time he wasn't going to let her go so easily. The only woman he wanted a family with was Ali.

## 7 Sheriff Visit

Grant finished his last bite of pancakes when Milan rushed into the kitchen. We have a black SUV headed our way. The camera that I posted near the first gate caught the vehicle.

Ali went to her room to hide her clothes in the drawers. She quickly made the bed and checked the bathroom one last time. Taking her white jacket, ski pants, and sweater, she disappeared into the special closet in her room. The space was a secret compartment for expensive jewelry and papers. Not too many people knew the space existed. Grant designed and built the space.

Milan moved her car into his two-car garage the first day she arrived. The brothers checked the living room for glasses, blankets, and pillows. The laundry room was cleaned yesterday, and the room was sparkly clean.

"You know the drill, Milan. Let's keep ourselves calm."

The knock alerted the men to the fact that the sheriff arrived quickly to their door. Grant opened the wooden door, letting a gust of wind into the house.

"Morning, sheriff, isn't this a nice day and I might add, very early surprise."

"Well, by golly, Grant, when did you arrive home? I came to see if Milan was okay. I saw some of the cows in the lower field chawing on the weeds. Usually he has moved them to the water tank with some hay."

Milan put his dishes in the sink. This was the perfect opportunity for him to exit the house and do his morning chores.

"Excuse me, I have to run. Nice to see that someone checks on our cows."

Grant extended his hand to the sheriff, picked up the spatula, and turned back to the stove.

"Sheriff Cray, would you like some sausage, eggs, and pancakes," commented Grant as he slid a large cup of coffee to him.

"Don't mind if I do? You boys always seem to have enough food on hand for breakfast. My wife runs out of everything. I'm constantly going to the store to get bread and milk. I haven't had any peanut butter for seven years because those kids devour the stuff."

Grant laughed and grabbed the jar of peanut butter out of the cupboard and the strawberry jam from the refrigerator. He plunked both down on the counter.

"You still haven't answered my question," said the sheriff with his mouth full of pancakes.

"I arrived a couple days ago so that I could ride over to Johnson's ranch. I'm interested in purchasing some or all his acreage. He hasn't wanted to sell in the past, but I hear his daughter is sick."

"Yeah, she doesn't have any health insurance so I'm assuming her medical bills are mounting up. Johnson will want to handle her medical expenses."

Grant nodded and waited for the sheriff's next question. He braced himself on the high stool and then remembered to relax. He told himself to go slow with his answers.

"There's also another reason that I stopped by. You and Ali Zarin dated some years back. I assume you have listened to the news that she is missing, and a friend of hers has been murdered. The police are looking for Ali for questioning. A Detective Candace Moon contacted me late last night."

"This is the detective on the murder case in Aspen?"

"Detective Moon received your name from Ali's mom when the police interviewed the woman yesterday. The mother hasn't heard a word from her daughter. The mother told the detective that she didn't talk too much with her daughter and hadn't seen her for three years. However, she was able to tell the detective your name and the city where your ranch is located. Ali must have talked to her mother about you."

"Yes, I believe Ali did call her mother once while she was visiting with me. I'm surprised she remembered us."

Sheriff Cray saw Grant make a new pot of coffee.

"If Ali's still alive, I thought she might show up on your spread. The assumption by me is a normal one. The two of you were friends and lovers. You cooked a barbeque for your friends. You invited me and Matlock to the pig roast. At this barbeque, I was able to talk with Ali and get to know her. I was impressed with her straightaway. She's smart and capable of handling difficult people. I figured you were one of those difficult people after she went back to Los Angeles."

"We have had a difficult time. Perhaps I'm as bad as Milan with women."

"Stubborn is more like it. You two boys don't understand women. They get their way every time."

Grant shook his head.

"If I'm stubborn, you're cranky."

"Still, there begs an important question that I need to ask. If I don't, Detective Moon will be here in your face. I'd rather it was me. I know she's prettier, but I'm an old friend. Have you seen her?"

There was no hesitation in Grant's response. He'd rehearsed his answer in his mind.

"No, sheriff."

Grant poured himself a new cup of coffee and stirred in the cream, taking his time to continue to formulate a reply. He placed the pot within the sheriff's reach.

"I wish that I could help you. Ali and I parted ways, and we aren't exactly sociable anymore. She would rather see me dead than be here with me. If I recall her last words, it was something like she'd rather go to bed with a rattlesnake than live in my house. How dare I ask her to leave her precious career to become a cowgirl? Most women would be glad to live on my ranch."

"Ha, ha. You made me laugh. I bet her comments about your precious ranch also made you quite mad, especially after all the hard work that went in to building this place. It sounds like you are still sore at her," chortled the sheriff.

The sheriff lifted his to-go mug and Grant acknowledged the coffee was free today.

"Cowgirls get dusty boots around here, and that isn't all that's on the ground. Ali is pretty and fancy. It's too bad the pretty ones always get away. I don't think she killed her friend. There's no reason for a murder. She would use her mind to figure out a different way to get what she wanted."

Grant looked out the living room window. He was surprised at the sheriff's comments.

"No, I don't think she killed anyone either. Let's hope she escaped from the killer. Despite our differences, I wish her well and hope she's alive. Ali lived all over the country with her mom who was an Army nurse. She knows many small and large cities. Fear does bring most people down. However, she's resilient but her trust level is more than likely shaken."

The sheriff smeared peanut butter and jelly on his pancake, rolled the sweet cake, and dipped it in runny egg yolk. The sausage was wolfed down with the pancake.

"So, you believe she escaped from the killer. I could see her doing exactly that move. Her adrenaline and logic would kick in. She would wisely choose her next direction. If there was a killer tracking me, I'd face him. Women run and attack later. I wish I could catch the creep with the silencer. A good old-fashioned ambush would be the best situation. Drop the son-of-a-bitch to his knees. See how he likes to feel fear. Then let the buzzards have him."

"You believe the killer is a man?"

"Absolutely. There's my gut feeling about the tree line attack, sneaky and clever. He waited until it was almost dark and put a face mask on. He dressed like the ski patrol people. People saw the man and dismissed him. My gut is never wrong about evil."

Grant was pleased he made extra breakfast this morning. He regretted not making enough hash browns. Milan ate most of the potatoes.

Grant looked at the sheriff and smiled. They were both in agreement regarding the killer. The other woman's death didn't sit well with either of them. There was a killer loose and no one knew where. The sheriff was an old friend except there were private items Grant wouldn't share until the timing was right. Revealing Ali's whereabouts was one of those private items. Grant wanted to catch the killer.

The sheriff noted Grant's silence. He stayed long enough. The boy obviously still held special feelings about Ali. He also knew Grant hated bad people and murderers as much as he did. They talked a long time several years ago when Milan got into some trouble with a bad gang.

"Well, thanks for breakfast. I'll be getting down the road. However, if she does make contact, you have my number. Would you mind if I used your facility? I need to make a rest stop."

Grant motioned toward the bathroom. He knew the sheriff was going to peak into the bedrooms. He picked up the dishes and started rinsing them at the sink before putting them in the dishwasher. The kitchen was almost clean when the sheriff finally reappeared.

Grant walked him to the door, and they said their goodbyes.

The sheriff was full and happy when he drove down the ranch road and saw Milan watering the herd. He felt good that the visit was over. Grant even refilled his coffee mug for him.

The sheriff was pleased to know the Evans boys were doing well. He'd have to let his wife know about old man Johnson and the possible sale. She liked to keep up with the local news. He wondered if he could buy a jar of strawberry jam and keep it in the vehicle, away from his kids. Maybe he'd buy some soda crackers. They would fit in the glove compartment.

His thoughts wandered. He saw the ravens chasing lizards in the desert. Now he could send the nosy Detective Candace Moon a note stating he checked out the property and talked with the owner. There was no sight or contact with Ali Zarin. They all hoped she was still alive somewhere else.

The sheriff headed his vehicle towards his office and computer. Maybe he could get the receptionist to help him put the note together. He wasn't that good a speller. The receptionist would know where to put his signature, Sheriff Andrew Cray. He was proud of his name, good at his job, and a twenty-year police veteran. The sheriff didn't want any females stepping on his toes in his own territory.

"No, siree, we have enough trouble without foreigners crawling all over the place."

# LINDA MCKOWN

The sheriff called everyone foreigners if they didn't live in his state as did his friend, Matlock. The two older men were a rare and different breed. They loved their country and weren't afraid to defend it or its citizens. The men rode their horses in the local Fourth of July parade. Their spurs and guns were polished. Their horses were immaculate.

The older men knew the law sometimes got bent a little. The sheriff wanted Ali to lay low. She'd be safer around Grant's place. The sheriff would make a call to Matlock to update him on the current situation. There would be a showdown in the future.

## 8 Taxidermist's House

**Detective Candace Moon** waited for her partner, Doug Constantine, to arrive from his flight. They were going to meet at the car rental agency. She wasn't too excited about meeting the next person on their list. Latin Dooley lived in Indian Springs outside of Vegas.

Detective Moon reread her notes about the interview with Ali's mother. She would share them with her partner on the drive north.

Ali's mother told Candace that they knew Latin as a teenager when they lived in Las Vegas. Ali and Latin were close and played together. There was one particularly crazy incident when the mother drove fifty miles from their home to pick up Ali. Ali called her from a gas station. Her tennis shoes were muddy, and her clothes looked like Ali fell in the woods. Ali wouldn't tell her mother what happened. She only mentioned Latin was stupider than a dead raven. Ali no longer was his friend. Latin was dead to her.

The mother forgot about the incident because they moved away two weeks later. Ali became ill with the mumps right before they left town. The mother told the detective it was a horrible time for both.

The mother's new jobs kept her busy. Ali was left alone most of the time. Her mother never knew where Ali went nor any of her friends. Then Ali went to college and moved away from home permanently. Ali was friends with Lisa Givens in college. The two women knew each other during their college years.

They went their separate ways and obtained jobs in the news media. Ali used everyone. Lisa was used as a reference for Ali to get into KMDZ-LA10 in Los Angeles.

The detective asked Ali's mother what she meant by her daughter used everyone. The mother's response was a negative shrug. The detective was told to go ask Ali's co-workers. The mother didn't seem to care too much about her daughter. They, obviously, weren't close.

Candace was anxious to see Doug's report. She might need to re-interview the people at KMDZ-LA10 in Los Angeles. There may be more areas to investigate, especially if Ali was disliked by fellow employees. There may be other people than this crazy Latin who disliked Ali when she was younger.

Candace hated being in Nevada. Her ex-husband lived in Tonopah in a house that cost one hundred thousand dollars. She googled the street her ex-husband lived and knew she would never go there.

Doug finally arrived and Candace filled her partner in regarding Ali's mother. Doug relayed his information from the Los Angeles interviews. Candace wasn't pleased with his notes which put her in a feisty mood for their interview.

The house of Latin Dooley was older. Instead of siding, there was brown shingle material that looked like bricks on the exterior. The gray paint was peeling around the windows. An upper floor window was cracked. The weeds were an odd assortment of dried flower heads. Bushes were overgrown and a few dead trees were in the backyard. She saw the LP tank on the other side of the house. There was a newer white van sitting in the driveway next to the small garage.

Doug said, "You could fit a body in that van."

"I wonder why Mr. Dooley doesn't park the van in the garage. Too bad the windows are tinted. We can't properly see inside. His yard's not seen a landscaper in years."

Doug tried the doors of the vehicle.

"They're locked. Landscapers cost money."

Candace saw the mailbox by the door. The box was old and dirty. The house numbers were peeling off the metal.

"Maybe he has neighbors that don't like him."

"He probably shoots his neighbors." Doug pointed at the rusted stop sign that contained bullet holes.

Candace and Doug knocked on the porch screen door. No one came. Doug opened the screen and they walked onto the decrepit porch. There was a door buzzer. Doug pushed on the antique bell.

They heard a commotion inside and swearing.

Latin Dooley arrived at the door. Candace and Doug showed their badges and introduced themselves.

Reluctantly, he let the two detectives into his home. He was always nervous about people seeing his prizes on the walls, so he first pulled the doors almost shut.

Latin was a small man, slightly bent over, with a wisp of black hair. His nose appeared broken at some point in his career. His clothes were clean. There were

66

piles of old newspapers and magazines stacked on the floor.

Latin moved a few piles and the detectives sat down. Candace noted the age of the furniture. The couch was a maroon velvet. She felt the cushion which was hard as could be.

Doug quipped, "Horsehair."

Candace's eyes grew wide.

Latin responded. "The couch was my mother's and the dump wanted seventy-five dollars to haul away. I never sit on the thing. The couch gives me a backache."

Latin offered the detectives some water. Doug made the mistake of accepting. Latin went off to bring a glass of water back into the room. There was a tiny chip on the rim.

During his absence, they could hear him pumping the water into the sink. Candace and Doug took the opportunity to peer into the rooms. They were surprised to see mostly stuffed birds and several raccoons.

Latin caught them coming out of the trophy room. "The raccoons were pests in my garbage cans. They needed to be gone from this earth. I tried the BB gun. Next the rifle was shot. That's when the sheriff told me I had to stop shooting the stop sign cause of the neighbors. My brain figured rat poison would work. The sheriff never said anything about the missing raccoons."

# RAIMENT RED AND A RAVEN

Doug took the glass and when Latin wasn't looking, he poured the offering into a dried cactus plant. Latin would figure out next week where the water went when the cactus bloomed. In the meantime, Doug was glad to dispose of the glass on a nearby coffee table filled with more dried plants. The detective nicked his finger on a spike and put his white handkerchief over the spot.

"Isn't killing raccoons illegal within the city limits?" said Doug.

Latin knew the law. The smart-alecky, young detective was trying to remind him of those facts.

"My neighbors complained about animals and birds missing. They found out that I was a taxidermist. The raccoons' mouths foamed. I told the second officer the animals had rabies. It was my life or theirs."

Candace smirked and decided to take over the meeting.

"Why were you registered as a guest at the Aspen ski lodge at the time of Lisa Given's murder?"

"I was there to see Ali Zarin. I hoped she would talk to me. I brought my raven along so she could see how beautiful he still was."

"You brought a live raven into the hotel without telling the desk clerk?"

Latin looked exasperated. "No, they charge for live animals. I brought a stuffed raven to show her how nice a re-do job would look. I brought the same raven we played with in Vegas."

Candace looked at Doug. The message sent between them was *nut case*.

"Did you ever get to talk to Lisa or Ali while you were in Aspen?"

"No, I just got there the day of the photo shoot."

Doug handed the bill from the lodge for the duration of Mr. Dooley's stay.

"Well, maybe it was the day before. I forget days and things. The two women weren't at the lodge. They were staying in a rental. The lodge was crowded and next thing I know, there were cops crawling all over the place. Cops interfere with guests and ask stupid questions. Now I don't mind your questions. Detectives do much better. I checked out as did many other guests. People were worried for their safety. I was worried. I did nothing wrong."

"Did we say you did something wrong?"

"You are here, aren't you? You only visit people who you think are responsible. I don't need no one hassling me."

"Did you ever want to hurt Lisa Givens or Ali Zarin in any way?"

Mr. Dooley jumped up from his chair as if a piece of buckshot hit him.

"I shouldn't have let you in my house. You think that I'm strange. I'm not the person who has some black marks on their career. If Ali's company knew what I know, they wouldn't have promoted her. Ali was the strange one. She stepped on people. She used her body to get promoted. I've heard stories."

Doug recognized paranoia and took over. "We are investigating a murder and disappearance. We are questioning everyone from the hotel and anyone who knew the two women. We have your name from a card that you gave Lisa and from the hotel register. We thought you would feel more comfortable in your own home with our interview. Ali is missing so I'll ignore those last remarks. She isn't here to defend herself. We understand she did some modeling while in college. Modeling bras and underwear isn't a crime."

"She went to Japan for the underwear gig. What do you think happened there? I can only guess."

"How did you know she went to Japan?"

It was Latin's turn to smirk. "I read Japanese and buy some of their magazines. I would recognize Ali any day of the week."

"How did you become acquainted with Lisa Givens?"

"I watch the news and figured she could help me contact Ali."

"Lisa probably didn't want to help you. Did her lack of support piss you off and make you mad?"

Latin's lips were a straight line. "No. I was upset when she didn't call me. I called their company. They told me most of the employees were in Aspen. I flew there. I saw the women leave to go skiing. I'm not stupid. They had no time for me that evening. I was going to wait and try again. You see I wasn't mad. Do the police know where Ali is located? I do need to talk to her about a message that she might have received erroneously. It's very important."

"Did you see anyone following the two women?"

"No."

Candace was tired of the negatives.

"Please tell us what is in your message and when the message was delivered."

"You give me no information and you want me to tell you things. How nosy and unkind? The message is my affair. There's nothing for the cops or their police detectives."

"This message could be considered evidence."

The little man suddenly changed.

Candace stood up and looked at the little man sitting in the chair. His eyes were beady like a raven. A chill crossed through Candace as she saw him in her mind delighted in tearing flesh on dead birds or using a knife.

"Your knives are locked away I will assume. We saw them in the glass cabinet. Do you own any guns?"

"Yes, to the knives which you've both seen while snooping in my house and no, to the guns."

Candace saw Latin glance at one of the rooms. He kept his knifes and other taxidermy paraphernalia in this one room. She thought about a search warrant. The judge would need more cause. Latin was not being truthful with them. He knew something or had done something. She believed both scenarios were possible.

In that moment, Candace knew Latin was somehow connected to the killer. Much like the New Mexico sheriff, her instincts proved right on. She just didn't know how this clever man fit into the murder. Why did she believe he was clever? Candace ran across

71

all types of criminals and this one played dumb. The twitch of his mouth was her first clue and the way he rubbed his hands. The man was tightly controlled. At this point in the investigation, she didn't want to scare him off. There was much more detective work to find out the truth.

"If we have any updates, the information will be released to the public. I see you do have a 50-inch screen TV with cable. If you think of anything further, here is my card."

Latin eagerly jumped up from his chair to lead the two detectives to the door. The soured interview was over. Latin wanted to spit but would wait until the detectives were gone.

Doug turned to the suspect, almost toppling the little man.

"Oh, Mr. Dooley, we forgot to tell you not to take any vacation out of the area until our investigation of the murder is over. Fifty miles should give you plenty of room to get more rat poison. You might want to buy some paint for your garage. Black would cover soot nicely. And I would keep your biases about a different nationality to yourself."

Candace told Doug her thoughts about Mr. Dooley.

"Latin knew the women were staying in a rental. I wonder how he came across that information?"

"Do you think he met Lisa?"

"I don't know."

Doug was on the same page with Latin as a suspect. They boarded the airplane for Los Angeles. Both detectives knew they would be back to visit Mr.

Dooley. Next time there would be a search warrant for possible weapons.

Candace pondered about the message erroneously delivered.

"Did Ali have the message or was the message an object? Was she still alive? Her mother thought she was alive."

Candace typed in her laptop computer on the airplane. Doug was fast asleep beside her. She couldn't sleep. The puzzle kept her wide awake. There was also a connection to Lisa Givens and Latin Dooley.

"But where was the connection? Of course, the card. Was there a meeting before the card? Who first contacted whom? Latin never married and there doesn't appear to be any men friends. Ali caught the mumps when she knew Latin. I wonder. Revenge is always possible. Backfire happens."

Her brain kept circling. The bag of pretzels was gone. She reached into Doug's pocket to eat his packet. She was developing a headache. Reaching for her aspirin bottle, she stopped and put the bottle back into her purse. She pressed the button for the steward. She was buying a beer. Doug awoke when the steward approached.

"Make that two beers."

Doug smiled that she was buying. After this case was solved, she was going on vacation. A note came across from the office. Candace quickly opened the file labeled Lisa Givens autopsy report. She read through the document, closed the file and shut down her computer.

The two beers arrived with more pretzels.

Doug raised his glass, "Let's toast to our solving this case."

"Not so fast, Sherlock. Lisa Givens was three months pregnant. We have bigger problems added to the murder mystery because no one from our investigation came forward with this piece of news. There's more than one person hiding information. How did you know that was soot on Mr. Dooley's garage? I thought it was dirty oil."

Doug said, "I called a fireman friend of mine. He got my text with the photo of the back end of the garage. Latin contacted the fire station here."

"What happened?"

"I'm hungry. I know this place that makes the most fantastic hamburgers with pickles, barbeque sauce, and cheese. We could go have a meal together and I'll explain. What do you think?"

Candace heard this line a lot from her partners. She was curious about Latin's garage. Carefully, she approached the dinner date. "I'm hungry. I do like late night burgers with a friend. The only other problem is who sleeps on the couch?"

Doug thought a moment. "I can sleep on the couch."

"Good, then I accept the hamburger date."

"I kind of like that word date. It evokes more opportunity to come."

Candace shook her head. "Don't push it."

"Absolutely not," commented Doug. He was grinning as she gently squeezed his hand.

## 9 Ben and Bicycle Courier

**The receptionist at** KMDZ-LA10 called Ben Blake's office. "The two detectives have asked to speak with you. I'll be sending them to the elevator. They will meet you in your office."

"What two detectives? Oh, the same guy, Doug, who was here the other day?"

"Yes, his name is Detective Doug Constantine and Detective Candace Moon."

"Does Mr. Fleming know about their visit?"

"The CEO is out today attending another local golf tournament."

Ben was unhappy about talking with the detectives. There was no way to get out of the interview. The receptionist pointed the two detectives toward the elevator.

Ben welcomed his visitors and took them to a conference room so the whole office wouldn't hear their conversation.

Candace sat down next to Ben and Doug was on the other side.

"Can I get you some coffee or water?"

"Coffee with cream would be nice."

Ben pushed a button and asked the administrative person to bring coffee.

"Well, I feel surrounded by the law. Mr. Fleming and our lawyer should be here as witnesses. They are both golfing today. Therefore, I guess I'm your man. What brings you to my desk?"

# LINDA MCKOWN

Candace said, "Doug talked with the accounting department regarding the expenses for the Aspen photo shoot where Ali Zarin modeled. Much to our surprise, there were no entries for payment to Star Magazine. Per Mary, sometimes contracts and payments are sent via a bicycle courier company. You're the person who arranges for the courier pickup and deliveries. You then turn in the charges to accounting who pays the clients involved in the transaction. Mary assumed you were holding the receipts due to the circumstances your company now faces with a loss of two employees. Did you arrange a delivery to this magazine?"

"No, I did not."

"But you did send fifty thousand dollars to Celebrity Consultants to hire three people from Star Magazine for some freelance work. The three people were Mike Smith, cameraman; Josh Jones, lighting and director; and Cameron Day, props person. They arrived a day before the murder and stayed in the rented cabin's bunk room. Josh Jones stayed at the lodge with his teenage son. We understand the son was a helper with the raven."

Candace watched Ben fidget with his watch and continued.

"After completion of the photo shoot, the men waited for the director and left to go to the airport. The three people were on the same flight back to Los Angeles and Ali's boyfriend took a flight to New York. Per their statements, the film crew never acted under the magazine's name nor did they mention their employer's magazine. Lisa was the one who kept referring to the magazine during the scenery set. However, the three men's employment has been terminated by Star Magazine because of their outside involvement and bad press. The magazine does not want the responsibility or blame in a lawsuit over a murder."

"Wow, I guess you have been checking out people. Are the three freelancers now suspects?"

Doug decided to take over. "Look, are you playing stupid? You're the one in trouble for hiring these people and for the creation of the photo shoot. A person in your company was killed. Where did you get the funds? Are you holding the receipts to bury your tracks or someone else's? Maybe you had Ms. Givens murdered?"

"No, oh no, not me. I'm only a worker who does what he is told. I wouldn't kill a fly. You can't blame me for this mess. I told Lisa the photo shoot was not a good idea. I told our boss the same thing. No one believed me. I'm not stupid. We all know Ali has a temper. Everyone could hear her whenever she was displeased which was most of the time. I know Ali looks pleasant on the news, but you didn't have to work with her. And there was Lisa. She was snoopy."

"Did Lisa pay for the photo shoot or your boss?"

Ben nervously tapped his pen on his notebook. "The package was sitting on my desk with instructions signed by Gene Fleming. I have a copy of the letter in my desk. I entered the information in my journal log."

Candace rubbed her forehead. "Did you ever open the package?"

"No. I assumed there was cash, a check, or something else inside. The company didn't want me to see. That's why it was sealed. Someone stamped private on the package. I know not to open them."

"Did anyone in the office see the package?"

Ben stopped his tapping. "Lisa was snooping around my desk and saw the large envelope. She looked pleased. Obviously, she kept our CEO wrapped around her finger. She was pleased about the photo contract."

"Why did your CEO and Lisa want to setup the photo shoot if there was no magazine cover attached?"

"I'm not sure. They both said something about a show where they would reveal later to Ali the news that the cover was a prank. They would do this on the air. You know, like a joke, to raise ratings. Lisa thought up the idea. I think she wanted a promotion out of the raise in ratings. Mr. Fleming seemed okay with the deal. Lisa paid another five thousand dollars in cash to a different company for the live bird. That package was not marked private."

"Was the bird mentioned in your approval letter from the CEO?"

"No, the bird came later. The handler seemed like a friendly guy when I talked with him about the contract. I assumed the payment was all right. I'm not in trouble here, am I? The payment was legal, wasn't it? I'm not going to lose my job over this? I didn't know anyone was going to be murdered or kidnapped. Maybe you should talk to Mr. Fleming."

Doug looked at Candace. "We don't know if Ali has been kidnapped. We hope not. We need the name of the bird handler. By the way, don't go anywhere. We'll type up your statement and have you sign it within the next hour."

"You mean I don't have to go back to work."

"Not until we are done. However, I will need the CEO approval letter, the bird contract, and the finished photographs. I believe the photographs arrived today and there are ten proofs in the mail room. The outside lettering stated *don't bend the ten photos inside.*"

Ben stood up. "I haven't checked my mail. I'll be right back." He scrambled down the hall.

Doug ran after Ben to the mail room and his desk. They didn't trust Ben and his closeness to a shredder. Evidence disappeared when detectives were on a company's floor.

Ben came back with the unopened photo package and approval letter.

"Doug's typing at my desk. Do I get to see the photos while we wait?"

Candace just stared at Ben who was sweating. She wasn't sure the sweating was from his recent exercise.

Ben whined, "What am I supposed to tell Mr. Fleming about your interview and taking the photographs? I'm sure he will be displeased."

"Don't worry. We'll handle the package with care. Although there are times when we do divulge information to the public via the news media."

"Oh, no, you wouldn't let the media see our photographs. Mr. and Mrs. Fleming would be upset. Our company could use the photographs to help the police," said Ben.

Doug came back into the conference room and handed his computer to Ben. "Go ahead and sign on the line with your finger."

"I should read the document first."

Doug told him every little detail was in the document exactly as presented.

Ben gulped and signed the document.

Doug and Candace left to talk to their boss at police headquarters.

"Did Ben appear to be nervous to you. He acted strange about the package. For someone who handles packages and outside company dealings, you would think a question about packages would be a simple request. He also acted strange and mentioned Mrs. Fleming. I thought Mrs. Fleming let her husband handle their business affairs."

Doug shook his head. "I thought the man was totally strange just like this courier arrangement. People use other means of communication and banking methods like wire transfers. I didn't understand him mention Mrs. Fleming. Your point is interesting."

The news media would be all over the new revelation in the case that the CEO and Lisa Givens arranged the business transactions to enhance news ratings.

The detectives looked at the photos of Ali and picked the one with the raven. Ali was looking directly in the bird's eyes. The picture would accidentally get published. Detective Moon knew a reporter, Alicen Stone, who took a photo of a file when Ali stepped out of her office. The folder was left purposefully in plain sight with one specific photo. Ali would be a star in a newspaper for one day.

The detectives hoped the photo would flush either the killer or Ali out of hiding. The photograph was worth a shot.

Doug grabbed the pile of photographs to put them back into the envelope. One photograph showed a closer view to the left of the model.

"The woods in the photo contains something weird."

Candace looked.

"There's a man in the woods watching Ali."

"A possible stalker?"

"Why would there be one?"

Doug made a gesture in the air, "Ali is popular as a news person. We might have a possible fan in the picture."

"The man is stooped down. Have our camera people see if they can get a cleaner image."

Doug put the photograph in between pages of his notebook.

"I'll give the camera person the item today."

## 10 News Update on Murder

**The police released** a statement regarding newly presented evidence in the murder case of Lisa Givens. They confirmed Ali Zarin's goggles found later at the scene contained Lisa's blood. Also, the collusion of the company in rigging a photo shoot was revealed.

A photo of Ali hit the newspaper on the same day. The newspaper hoped by releasing the photograph, they would reach all areas of the country besides LA. If anyone noticed Ali, they were to contact the newspaper or police with her whereabouts. The police were worried for her safety and wanted to question the woman. The newspaper reminded the public a killer was still at large.

The news media vans were parked outside KMDZ-LA10's headquarters waiting for the CEO, Gene Fleming to explain why he created the fake photo shoot with Ali Zarin that resulted in one of his employee's death. The media were now suspicious of the CEO and what else his company or he were hiding from the public and the police.

Other people joined the news crews and the scene developed into an angry mob. Security was called to push back the crowd so the CEO and his wife could leave the building.

Upon their appearance, the crowd pushed forward, trapping Mr. Fleming and forcing him to answer a few questions.

"Mr. Fleming, sir, were you aware of the photo shoot payment and were company funds used? We heard the package was given to Ben to handle the fake enterprise."

"Yes, I knew of the photo shoot. It was Lisa Given's idea. She brought five thousand dollars to the table for the bird. The deal with her was that our company would pay Lisa back with interest if our ratings rose. Also, there was a large bonus for Lisa in the deal. I didn't tell the police initially because my company felt the photo shoot had nothing to do with her death. We gravely miss Lisa and sincerely hope to find Ali. We want her back with our company again."

Mr. Fleming made a move for a few steps and was trapped again by another reporter.

"Sir was there any romantic business going on between you and Lisa Givens. A photo of the two of you was found in her desk."

Mr. Fleming's face turned pale white and his wife's turned beet red.

"That statement is absurd. The photo of Lisa and I was from a company outing attended by half my staff. I've never had an affair with any of my co-workers. You're a disgrace as a reporter. I know your boss and I will file a complaint with him. Now get out of my way."

Slowly, the security guards deposited Mr. and Mrs. Fleming in their vehicle so they could leave the company grounds.

"That's a wrap from our station, but we still have many questions. Does Mr. Fleming know of Ali's location? Is he financing her disappearance like the bogus photo shoot? As you can see, his company is getting a lot of attention over Lisa Givens' death and Ali Zarin's disappearance. We must wonder if the gig was worth the increased ratings. We hear other people at a magazine were fired for their involvement in this nasty business. This is reporter, Alicen Stone, with KPPG-CA07."

Grant Evans clicked off the television set. Ali sat stone still. She was overwhelmed by the story and the photo.

"I very much liked the photo with the raven. You might get that cover in a magazine after all. I would buy the magazine."

Ali knew that Grant was trying to sooth her disappointment. She should be extremely angry.

"For some reason, I don't care anymore about my job, my life, my picture. Everything seems small and petty. I only know one thing and that is to present the news."

"You're wrong. You have lots of other skills. I've seen you throw a rope at a cow and lasso her neck tight. See, I made you smile."

Ali moved off the couch and went into the bedroom. Grant followed.

"I need to pack a few things and go back to Los Angeles to my company. I can't believe they arranged the mess."

"You just said that you didn't care about your job. I'm confused. Besides, if you go back, it will be like walking into a bear's den."

"You mean lion's den."

Grant was frustrated. "Lion, bear, what does that matter. The killer is still out there. The police might believe that you got angry and killed Lisa. Your goggles have her blood. That Ben guy said you were always angry in the office in the statement the police read. Maybe you got mad at Lisa."

"I never liked Ben. He never liked me. Hence, his statement. He calls women bitches. I bet everyone is laughing about the photo shoot at the office. It would be difficult to go on the air and remain composed. I'd either be mad or sad. My apartment building would be surrounded by news vans. You're right, the police might arrest me. Now is not a good time to make my entrance."

"Good because I've arranged to stay two more weeks with you. I can't leave you here unprotected."

"Is that what you call what you are doing. I thought you were my cook and dishwasher."

Grant gently enfolded her in his arms. "Someday you will be nice to me."

"Let me go. I'm having a hard time being this close to you."

"No, I rather like touching you."

Grant made a move to kiss Ali and she quickly stepped away.

"I can't do this with you right now. I have to figure out what to do next."

"All right. Then we'll help. What do you think the murderer is doing today after seeing the news?"

"He's probably more worried that I'll be found."

"In that case, I believe we should move you to the cabin in the pinyons. Not too many people know about my new place. I've been renovating the inside. Last year, Milan and I redid the outside timbers on the barn and put a new metal roof on the place. I can go with you and we can take some of the horses. Also, we'll need supplies, a vehicle, and more guns."

"You never told me about a cabin. I think that's a good idea. Does the sheriff know about the cabin?"

"Yes, he's been there. I believe he will not come there unless invited."

"You are that sure about the sheriff?"

"Yes, he's a friend. Matlock is first, the Evans boys are second, and the law is third."

"I liked the sheriff at the barbeque. Matlock, too. I remember the sheriff's wife. She brought jars of dill pickles and sweet peppers. They were in old peanut butter jars. When do you want to go?"

"As soon as we can load the horses and their gear in the trailer. I'll make a list of food stuff for Milan to purchase later."

"Do you need help with the horses?"

"No, you pack warm clothes and stay out of site. If you need more clothes or female stuff, we can order them online. We could use some ham sandwiches and coffee to eat on the road. Then we won't have to stop."

Ali went into the kitchen while Grant walked outside to the casita to talk with Milan.

Ali selected a pistol from the gun rack and her shells. The last time she shot a gun was at this ranch. Grant taught her all the safety features and how to handle a weapon. She would let Grant choose the other weapons. She wished they owned a dog. A dog would bark a warning. She looked outside at the security camera on the casita. She knew there would be security at the cabin.

"There's security at the cabin."

Grant was always well prepared.

## 11 Cabin in the Pinyon Trees

**The horse trailer** was ready. Ali was surprised to see four horses and a large truck in the driveway.

Grant said, "We always take four horses. For some reason, they love to trail ride and pasture there."

"How long before we arrive?"

"We'll take the back roads which are longer. Normally, it takes an hour and a half. The way we are going, we'll be on the road two hours. I think you will like the place. The land is higher in elevation and cooler. We've cleared around the home for fire safety and have the pasture cleared with a new barn for the horses and well. We've begun the riding trails which also will act as a break in the trees for fire stoppage. The well pumps water into a huge reservoir for us. We've bought our own graders, fire equipment, and helicopter."

"You fly a helicopter?"

Grant laughed, "Yes, the sheriff and I have been taking flying lessons together. He thought we needed one in case of an emergency."

Ali was quiet during the rest of the drive. Grant dropped her off at the house and went inside with her. He wanted to see her reaction. He loved the view more than the ranch one.

"Oh, look at all the pinyon trees. They are all green and breathtakingly beautiful."

"I'm glad you like the scenery. I'll get the horses settled and disconnect the trailer. You can check out the cabin and decide which room you want. Mine is the large one on the left."

Ali snooped around the cabin. She was surprised there were two stories and a round lookout tower. She could see part of the pasture and a large metal building at the middle left of the hill. This must be where they park the tractors and helicopter. The water tower was hidden behind the barn. She could see the trail ride runs.

Finally deciding on a room across from Grant's would work, she deposited her things. There were canned goods in the cupboard and some steaks and chicken in the freezer. She saw a box of powdered eggs and milk in the pantry. There were boxes of homemade biscuits, cornbread, and bread rolls.

"We won't be starving anytime soon."

The kitchen contained a pot rack of glistening copper pans.

"Expensive."

There were four large orange and white pieces of pottery on high shelves in the kitchen giving the place a southwest vibe. The clear glass canister with shiny silver tops held an assortment of chili peppers, beans, and salt. The other side of the kitchen held canisters with cinnamon stalks, whole nutmeg, and sugar. There was a wreath of various herbs, bay leaves and lavender on the wall.

"Alessandria's help, I'm sure. I have to admit, she has good taste in art, men, and spices."

She wandered into the vast family room and noted the artwork and wool textiles on the walls. The design was very southwest. Downstairs were more bedrooms, a billiard table, and a large wine refrigerator.

An impressive buffalo skin was on the wall. She touched the fur and was surprised how bushy the texture felt.

"Manly touch."

A saddle with silver trim sat on a built-in railing with a wool blanket. She liked the leather and striped blanket. The silver trim was recently polished. She knew Grant would keep the silver gleaming.

There were small pieces of firewood in a large copper bucket. An Indian leather headdress and spears adorned a different wall. She touched the spear.

"More manly stuff."

The two oil paintings in the rooms were large landscapes. The room could hold another one.

"The other picture should be lavender or purple. Otherwise, very skilled artists. I'm impressed."

The furniture at the ranch was rustic. She noted the furniture at the cabin was a higher quality burled wood. The finish told her pricey. Grant seemed to want the cabin to be his master show room of homes. She wondered why the elegance.

In the master bedroom, there was a silver framed picture set on the dresser. One picture was of Milan and she was surprised to see the other picture was of her and Grant on horseback. She remembered the day of the horse ride. They were herding the cows at the ranch to move them to the lower fields. Grant bought her a white cowboy hat. Ali fingered the frame and felt the past was a simpler time in her life.

The dressers and headboards in the master bedroom were burled oak with handmade wrought iron knobs and bars. The circle knobs contained the letter "E" for Evans. The hanging wrought iron chandelier was three tiers of lights. The dimmer switch on the wall toned the glare of light.

The drapery rods were wrought iron with beige linen drapes. They were lined. The bedspread was manmade grey fox fur with beige, brown, and purple Indian wool pillows. The large rug was grey, white, brown, and aqua-blue. The white sheets were expensive cotton. There were scented soaps in the bathroom. A vase of dried lavender added more fragrance. The rooms she saw held Grant's personality.

She went back to the wine bar, grabbed a red wine, and selected a white wine for their supper. She almost put the white wine back.

"I can trust Grant to be a gentleman. But do I trust myself? Hmmm, that's a very good question. Grant and his brother have certainly been busy while I was gone. Both men put their energies into this designer cabin."

Grant came back inside and saw that she put the steaks out on the marble counter to thaw plus a can of beans and corn with a cornbread box. He reached for the red wine and poured himself a glass. He saw the white wine was already open. He knew she saw the pottery in the kitchen.

Grant hoped she liked them despite the person who helped locate the pots for him to purchase.

Sauntering into the family room, she was reading one of the books he purchased about pine trees.

"Nice pots."

"Yes, they are and expensive, too."

"I imagined so. I believe the pottery enhances the ambiance in your kitchen. I approve."

Grant was glad she liked the pots. Seeing her in his cabin felt good. She fit in with the landscape. He dared not tell her that fact. Grant stared at the landscape outside the window for some time. He thought about some new building plans the architect was working on. He didn't tell Milan about his improvements to the cabin.

"You're awfully quiet. Are the horses inside or outside?"

"Outside for now. I'll bring them in before we cook our steaks on the outside grill."

"This cabin is amazing. I was thinking little."

"Since when have you known me to do anything little?"

Ali laughed, "Never."

He nodded in agreement. "I needed a way to get rid of all my hostilities after you left. I was pretty upset with you."

"I know. I'm sorry you were upset. My leaving was the right thing to do. We were at an impasse in our relationship."

Ali stopped talking.

Grant shrugged off his day dreaming.

"Now who's quiet. We are having a slow news day between us."

"Yes, there's much to discuss and I'm not in the mood."

Now Grant was angry.

"I'm in the mood to get this thing settled that's between us. I'll go first. Was I one of your *I don't care* packages? That's how I felt. What is with your boyfriend, Rad Newman? I saw him on the news after you were missing. He didn't seem sincere when he said that you' all should be fine, and he knew you were taking your time to reappear. Like, how would he know what you were doing or thinking?"

"He said you' all?"

"Ali, he's from Montana. They don't talk strange in Montana. They have real cow towns and buffalo. He even looks strange. I'm more handsome than he is and a lot smarter. Also, I talk normal to people no matter who they think they are."

"I know. Sometimes Rad can be obnoxious. He does travel and likes to mimic speech."

"If he's obnoxious, then why are you dating him?"

Ali laughed. "Temporary fun, like always."

'Hmmm. That's never a good idea. You didn't answer my question."

Ali sighed. "Are you handsomer?"

"No, not that one."

Ali knew Grant was distressed about the problem between them and the newer one. He also never liked her dating anyone else. The combative and competitive side of men always surfaced. Ali faced Grant.

"I was having problems with Rad. We were not connecting anymore. He wanted to break things off and I was feeling the same way. We skied together in Aspen. That's about all we did. He seemed to disappear in the evening. I gave up. There, you can stop worrying about the man. I already have. Isn't there a southern part to Montana?"

"No."

Ali sighed. "Let's try to be friends. I need your friendship right now. I can't deal with your being mad."

"I'm not mad at you. You date weird people lately. I'm good with your dropping Rad Newman. Now I can be a better friend."

"What did you tell Alessandria?"

Grant caught his breath.

"You heard the phone message she left at the ranch?"

"Accidentally, yes, I overheard. I didn't pick up and the recording replayed," said Ali.

"I explained to Alessandria that I appreciated her sympathy. Many people offered me their condolences here and at work. She didn't need to visit me in New York. I answered her questions with minimal answers. I told her I was handling my feelings about you like I always did. Life without you would be hard. I wanted my privacy respected. She backed off."

"I'm glad you didn't want her to visit."

Ali didn't comment about how Grant's life without her would be hard. She wondered if he meant those words or if he used them to halt a visitation from an unwanted guest.

Grant calmed down. He needed to switch the subject. Ali was here. Her closeness was what he needed. He didn't want to argue or be what the word was that the sheriff called him, stubborn.

Grant explained to Ali the cabin was at approximately 4500 feet above sea level. They hired a log company and contractor to build the structure. The contractor guaranteed the thermal windows, heavy insulation, and metal roof would work to block the high winds. The metal roof was for fire safety. They built stone structures by the patio areas to also minimize wind impact and to hide special fire hydrants that were hooked to the gray water cistern. Our landscapers used desert plants for screening and again to serve as wind breaks."

"I like the outside rafters and the purple mountain laurel bushes in clay pots," said Ali.

"The pots aren't clay. They are cement designed to look like ancient clay. We do receive snow at this elevation and the clay isn't strong enough. We tried some around the patio and they froze. We replaced those this year with white pots. They go well with the cactus, agave, and Bird of Paradise."

"I saw some of the grape vines by the hot tub. I loved the coral-pink sage."

Grant specifically asked for color on the back patio.

"There's various species of wildflowers down the hill's path. We have gardeners who come the first Tuesday of each month. You will need to stay out of their view for a couple of hours."

"No problem for me to disappear," said Ali.

"The pinyon tree nuts develop in September and October timeframe. You'll see the jays flying around trying to stuff as many nuts as they can into their mouths. The jays will bury them in the crooks of the trees. I work with a nut company whose crew comes out to harvest the bounty. They pick the nuts and haul them away. I get money in return. The nut-picking operation is something to see. I hope you will stick around to see the harvest. The company sends me a case of salted pinyon nuts at Christmas."

"The pinyon nuts sound interesting." Ali didn't respond to his request about staying. She wasn't sure about her future.

"There are conifer and juniper trees. We have a deal with a spice company for the juniper berries."

Ali said, "With all these trees and your cattle, it looks like the ranch and cabin pay for themselves."

"Yes, the ranch and cabin do fine each year in profits. I'm always looking for ways to expand and improve the numbers. I've reached the point where I need to hire permanent employees. I've talked briefly with Matlock. He's a good fit both places and someone I can trust. He might have some friends interested in applying. If we have additional people, we'll need to expand quarters for the workers and look at benefits like insurance to sweeten the deal."

"How can you do your lawyer job and this additional work?"

"Those are great questions. I'm looking at my options. I can always sell my condominium in New York. The realtor that approached me said the market was good."

Both drank their wine in silence. Ali went into the kitchen and made the cornbread. At the last minute, she dropped in a quarter cup of frozen corn and a dollop of sour cream into the mix. An extra egg was added next to the mix for richness.

Holding two pans, she debated about a loaf or muffin tin when Grant came into the kitchen. He brought out a black cast iron pan. "This one works best, but you need to butter the inside. No spray stuff on the black pans. The spray coats them with weird stuff."

"I didn't know. We'll try the cast iron."

Ali grabbed the honey and a dish of softened butter. She began stirring the concoction.

"Honey butter on cornbread. I haven't eaten that combination in years. Strawberry jam is my favorite."

"They say honey butter is the way to a man's heart. I know how to make strawberry freezer jam. I'll try to make a batch if you have jam jars. Do you want me to jazz up the beans like I used to do?"

"I would like your version of beans. It's one of the things that I missed about you. My heart will swoon when I eat tonight. The honey butter is a high. Yes, the jars are in the basement in a cupboard across from the laundry room. Marie, my housekeeper, bought a hodgepodge of jars. She is one of those women who doesn't know about plastic containers. She's thrown most of my plastic containers away. Marie told me the lids didn't match. I've hidden the freezer baggies in a drawer so she can't find them."

Ali shook her head and stopped mid-air wondering if her cooking was a good idea.

He saw her hesitation and dipped his finger into the corn batter for a taste.

"Needs some honey."

"No, it doesn't." Ali smacked him with her plastic spoon, getting batter on his shirt. He took the spatula away from her and spanked her rear.

She giggled and screamed for him to stop.

This time he wouldn't let her go. It was high time for him to make a move. Her lack of response about their future didn't set well. Yet, she talked about a way to a man's heart. Mixed signals were her trademark. Big moves were his trademark. They did him well in the business arena. With Ali, he fought for command. This time he would take the lead.

Grant stooped to kiss her. She didn't back away. The expensive wine lowered her defenses. He was encouraged and kissed her again. He stopped.

Ali raised her eyebrows.

"Later, I'm starved. We must cook the steaks before it's dark. The bugs come out. I also forgot to bring the yellow outside bulbs that I bought."

They cooked together and drank more wine. The dishes were thrown in the dishwasher and they both went into the larger bedroom. Ali decided she didn't need her old boyfriend. Decisions about her life could wait. She almost died. Dying gave a person a new appreciation for life.

"Tomorrow will happen soon enough."

"What did you say, Ali?"

"Good night."

"Yes, it was a good beginning to the night." Grant snuggled her body closer being careful of her wound.

"Did I tell you how beautiful you look?"

"Several times. Even though I'm scarred for life."

"Doctors can fix you. I'll buy."

"Hmmm, I might hold you to your words. You felt beautiful."

"How about I felt grand?"

"Grand and beautiful."

"I like those words very much."

Grant loved the sweet sounds she made when he held her close. Ali smiled and drifted to sleep. He could tell she was asleep. There was a slight snore.

She felt safe with him near. Her feelings for Grant were accelerating. The nightmare dream didn't happen. The reason might have been that Grant didn't let go of her all night.

In the morning, Ali felt more relaxed. Being with Grant was calming. They were old friends and she could be herself. The wound was healing, and she stopped worrying about infection. When the sun rose and the sky turned a soft blue, she almost forgot about her dilemma. Her step was lighter. She began to relax in the cabin environment. Cooking and recipes were her new focus as well as nights with a good lover. Grant paid attention to her and didn't disappear. If he did, she knew where he was most of the time. There was no need to worry.

## 12 Milan at the Cabin

**Milan's vehicle pulled** into the circular drive and stopped at the sprawling rock porch step. Ali and Grant helped unload the groceries. Grant put the freezer stuff away from the cooler and handed it back to Milan to return to the back of his vehicle.

He came back into the kitchen to see his brother, Grant, have his arm around Ali and they kissed.

"Wait, am I seeing correctly. The two of you are back together. Like, since when? Oops, none of my business. I'm glad some woman has finally saved his boots from rusting in their tracks. Why do I always get the wrong women chasing me?"

"You do need to mind your own business little brother. Why don't you take the roan horse out for a ride? She's been calling us all morning."

"There's a package you ordered for Ali while you were at the ranch. I'll go retrieve the bag."

Ali was curious what was in the bag. There were some warm black and white sweaters and slacks. Grant remembered her sizes and favorite colors. She was surprised to see some fuzzy black bedroom slippers. Ali complained about the cold floor in the morning in the kitchen. He told her that he ordered some more rugs.

"Thank you." She disappeared to put the clothing away.

Milan said, "I'll check the fences while I'm on the trail. The roan likes to snoop around the pine trees for bunnies."

"We'll take the other two and pack the third when we go for a short ride this afternoon."

"I'll take the pinto horse as a pack horse. This will make things easier if only the two of you go for a ride. She should wear my old coat and leather hat. That way, no one will notice her as a woman. Has Ali been updated on how to access the security cameras on our computers?"

"We're going to review the security now. I think she can wear her own gear. We are miles away from the main roads. If someone sees her, they might think we have hired ranch hands with their families."

Milan handed over the outdoor light bulbs he purchased. "I couldn't find the other ones you bought. Besides, I needed an excuse for Sheriff Cray. He saw the horse trailer go up the long hill."

Grant paced the wood floor. "Darn it. What else did you tell him?"

"I told him that you were staying at the cabin for a couple weeks to work on insulating the garage where we kept the helicopter. My job was to bring supplies and light bulbs. Then I was to get back to my cows. He seemed all right with the information. I looked and did not see him following my vehicle. I'll stay tonight in my room in the basement and leave about four in the morning."

"I did have the insulation delivered last time we were here. It's a good thing you remembered."

Milan frowned and Grant picked up on his brother's mood. Milan motioned for him to go downstairs with him and outside on the lower patio.

Ali was peeling carrots and potatoes. Their supper plan was roast beef stew. She kept eying the frozen bag small onions and peas on the counter. She would have to separate the onions and cook them first. The peas could go in last.

The brothers were out of ear shot from Ali.

"The sheriff passed some information from that female detective. He said that I should tell you because it might be important."

"Detective Moon is the female detective."

"Yeah, right. The autopsy report came back on Lisa Givens."

"Usually, the police release the information. I'll assume they are holding back for a reason."

"The sheriff told me the report showed she was three months pregnant."

"Pregnant. Ali was her friend and never mentioned those facts. I wonder if she knows and wonder who the father might be? Surely, the guy would have come forward by now."

"That's what the sheriff couldn't figure either. The two detectives on the case went to Ms. Givens funeral in the hope they would see or hear a confession. No male came forward or appeared overly distraught. The sheriff thought this was a strange development to the case. Are you going to tell Ali?"

Grant groaned. They were only beginning to get close again.

"Let me think about the pregnancy news. I'd rather she heard the information from me than the police or news media. I'll probably wait until tomorrow. I don't want to spoil this evening."

"Yeah, I get that you are a lucky man. I wish I held a hot woman in my bed while making love talk. My only scenery is horses and cows. Not much talking there."

"What happened to Lana?"

Milan shook his head. "She moved back to Florida. She missed her beach friends. I've been too busy to find somebody else."

"Well, thanks for bringing the supplies and information. Let's hope the sheriff doesn't decide to pay us another visit."

"Amen to that." Milan was going to the pasture to catch the roan horse. He grabbed a carrot off the counter.

"Hey," remarked Ali.

"Hay, that's what I need to bring into the barn. Thanks for reminding me, Ali. Boy, those onions cooking smell good. It's nice to have you cooking for a change. I like your food, even the fancy French sauce."

"Thanks, Milan. I also know how to cook Spanish dishes. I saw the chili peppers in the jar."

"Shoot, I was told by Alessandria the canisters were decoration. Oops, forget I mentioned her name."

"I'm all right. I listened to her message on the recorder before you erased the call. You told Grant about the message."

"Of course. Got to run and do my hay thing."

Milan was glad to escape the kitchen. He always said too much.

The evening was a pleasant one filled with memories of Ali's past visits. Milan told the two people the local news around the ranch. The next morning Milan was off early to return to the hacienda and ranch work.

Grant and Ali were done with their breakfast of thick polish sausage and scrambled Denver omelets. They were sitting on the upper porch drinking coffee. Grant decided there could be no secrets between them. He told her Sheriff Cray's information regarding Lisa. He could tell by her expression that she was unhappy with the news.

"I don't understand. Lisa should have told me. We used to be close. Lately, she was distancing herself from me. If I knew about the pregnancy, I wouldn't have requested she go on the last run. I killed her and a baby."

Grant touched her hand, "No, you did not kill them. The killer did those things. You have to stop blaming yourself."

"I wish I could turn back time. There's so much I would have said to Lisa."

"We all wish we could. Unfortunately, no one can. We must deal with issues as they hit us in the face. Our hope is the issue doesn't bring us down."

Ali held her cup letting the liquid warm her hands. "Who do you suppose the father might be?"

"Good question. I'm sure the same wonderment is bothering the police. They will try to find the answer. The other question is whether the killer knew."

"I hadn't thought of that piece. Do you think that's why she was killed? Was she the target and was I the person in the way? Interesting? So, there still is the other question, who would want Lisa dead?"

"The police are way ahead of you and me. This Detective Moon seems to be everywhere with this investigation. She keeps in contact with Sheriff Cray. I wonder about her digging around here in New Mexico. I think she sees me as a possible protector of women. As a lawyer, I know how far to push the law. Detective Moon understands the score."

"Do you believe she will show up here?"

"Eventually, yes. She needs more ammunition. Let's hope she finds the correct shells."

"Our danger is not from Sheriff Cray?"

"No, he will help us if we need him. I've always been able to count on the sheriff."

"Good," said Ali. "I need to lay down for a little while."

"Do you want me to join you?"

"I'm fine. I need some quiet time. Maybe this evening."

Grant went to the helicopter area and started putting the special insulation into the walls. He was whistling a love song.

# RAIMENT RED AND A RAVEN

# 13 Visit with Bird Man

**Detective Moon pulled** out her revolver and checked for bullets. Doug did the same. They were on some type of land called Wilderness Farms where there were caged animals of all types. Candace felt like she was at a zoo. She worried about the fencing. The caretaker assured them their fences were brought up to code. The caretaker brought them into the main building, and she went back outside to get the person they wanted to interview.

Hector Hansen walked into the building and sat down.

"I understand that the police have been looking for me. This is where I live in the winter. I bring my raven with me. Then I can continue the training. Ravens are very smart and most of the time, very lazy."

Candace asked him if she could see the raven that was at the photo shoot in Aspen.

"Sure, follow me outside. The bird area is over here." Hector held the raven for the detectives.

"Very pretty and raven-like. It's too bad you can't talk," said Candace.

"Thank you. The raven thanks you, too. They do have their own voice in the way of a caw. I imagine we should get back to the main area for your questions."

The raven pulled a piece of red netting from under its wing and held the netting in his mouth.

Hector became visibly angry. He tried to grab the netting and the bird would have none of it. The netting was the raven's treasure.

Candace said, "Oh, my, he does love red netting. Is that from Ali's dress?"

"I'm told the director brought a square piece of fabric out that appeared to match Ali's dress. The square was used to hide my leathers. The bird, I'm afraid, took a piece out of the fabric. The raven won't give the piece back."

"I think you would be wise to let him have his object of desire. You were not at the photo shoot in Aspen?" said Candace.

"I let the director's son handle the bird. He seemed to enjoy the raven. I waited at the lodge."

Doug followed his partner and Hector until they sat down in their chairs.

Detective Moon continued the interview. "The consulting agency told me they never used your company before this time, and that Lisa Givens recommended you. How did you know Ms. Givens?"

"Yes, I met Lisa Givens at a friend's home. She showed me his card. I knew the man. My friend is a little strange. When she heard we knew each other, she got excited. She wanted to meet there again to see my bird. I met her without the raven because I always carry a video. My friend is a little unusual and strange but has an impressive knowledge of birds and their behavior. He lives outside of Vegas in a relic of a house."

Candace looked at Doug.

"This person's name wouldn't be Latin Dooley would it?"

"Yes, how did you know? We match our wits against each other regarding bird facts. Currently, I'm ahead. We met quite a while ago at a bird convention in Vegas."

"We've been to his place recently questioning him regarding the same investigation. It's interesting that you took Lisa to see Mr. Dooley. He never mentioned those facts. Was she there previously before this visit, and was she ever left alone in the house while you were together?"

Doug acted with surprise by the detective's questions.

"I don't know if Lisa was there before. I never thought to ask her. Yes, Latin and I went outside to his garage. He wanted to show me a hole in the ground. He wasn't sure if it was a snake, tarantula, or lizard hole. We poured gasoline down the hole, threw the match, and poof. The snake came flying out. We almost burned the back of his garage down. There was smoke. We tried putting out the fire with two sets of hoses but gave up and called the fire department."

"How much time was Lisa in the house?"

"I'd say about forty-five minutes to an hour."

Doug raised the question. "Did you see Lisa again after the first visit?"

"Yes, she was in the lodge restaurant. I thought it odd we didn't meet at the rental where she was staying. She seemed nervous. For some reason, she didn't want anyone to know that we knew each other. I was fine. She already paid me money for the raven visit."

"Did you see Latin Dooley any time while in the lodge."

"No, I didn't know he was there."

"Why do you think Lisa was nervous?"

"I can't explain why. But then, I didn't know her very well."

"Have you talked to Mr. Dooley since the murder?"

"Yes, I did. He told me there was a handkerchief that belonged to an old friend that was missing after Lisa's visit to his home. The handkerchief was white with pink roses. He also said he thought his knife collection was messed with. The cabinet door was open. He didn't notice until after we left."

"Mr. Dooley believes Lisa took items from his home?"

"He didn't exactly accuse her. He only told me the one item was missing. I can't imagine why Ms. Givens would want anything or mess with his knives. She didn't seem the type to steal. Perhaps Mr. Dooley is getting old and senile."

"Old he is, but senile is not one of his traits," mentioned Doug.

"I think that I understand your meaning. Detectives, I don't think there is anything more I can tell you? My bird and I were fine with the gig. Not everyone likes ravens. The consulting agency apologized for Ms. Zarin."

"One more question. Do you know Ali Zarin?"

"I only know her from watching the news."

Does Mr. Dooley know anyone from Lisa Givens news station besides her and Ali Zarin?"

"I don't know. He did tell me that he was in Aspen to meet someone. There were many people from the news company at the lodge. Later Mr. Dooley told me he was messed up by the cops surrounding the place and I should ignore what he told me about Lisa."

"Interesting. The plot thickens. Did you meet Gene Fleming?"

"The CEO of the company? There was no reason to meet him. I'm hired help. Maybe Mr. Dooley and Lisa saw him. The lodge was heavy with people most of the time. There were many single people around in the evenings."

"Is there any good reason why Mr. Dooley hasn't married? It seems like his stuffed trophies are his children."

"He's sterile. He told me about a bad case of mumps when he was a teenager."

"Thank you for the bird show, your time, and information. We are done for now. I'll have Doug type up your comments. If you can wait five minutes, we'll get your signature on the statement and leave."

On the car ride, Doug asked her when they were going to interview Gene Fleming, CEO of the news station.

"Soon. I'm still formulating my questions. I believe he will have an alibi. I'm wondering how I can get a sample of his DNA without him noticing."

"I bet we can use the coffee cups we saw in the break room. The employees use the logo cups. I bet there's one in the CEO's room or their conference rooms," said Doug.

"Brilliant idea. The CEO was at the lodge the day of the murder. I understand he and his family are avid skiers."

Detective Moon nodded her head. Now she could look forward to the next interview.

"Were you getting any vibrations from Hector?"

Doug looked perplexed. "Now that you mention it, he seemed too nice. Ben said he was a nice guy. I wonder. Maybe we should check Hector's background. He was at the lodge in Aspen and knew the women stayed in a rental. He also knew Latin. I'm seeing a neat triangle of people who knew each other."

Candace took her time to decide. "Ali is outside the triangle, unaware of the other two people. Or unaware of Hector. Go ahead. Do the credit and background check on Mr. Hansen when you have time. We might see a pattern. We know where he keeps his raven in between gigs."

## 14 CEO Interview

**Detective Moon punched** the button on the small voice recorder to turn the machine on.

"Do you mind if we use this device? This will make it easier for Detective Doug Constantine to transcribe your statement."

"The device is all right if this will speed up the interview. I'm scheduled to pick up my new clubs. I'd like to try them out today. They've reserved a spot for me at the country club."

Detective Moon put down her coffee cup. She was glad to see Doug and Mr. Fleming held the same cups that contained the station logo.

The CEO was dressed in a navy-blue wool suit with matching pants. His silver hair was shorter, and his complexion tanned from hours in the sun. His white shirt and red tie were symbols of his executive status. Candace bet he wore matching golf shirts and shorts with a windbreaker. His golf gear would have to be upgraded every year. The limousine and corporate jet were more status symbols. She wondered how Gene and his wife met. Mrs. Fleming seemed to belong to the past century. Her husband was heavy into the present one.

Detective Moon did the introductions on the tape and started her questions.

"Our understanding is that you were at the lodge the day of the murder of Lisa Givens, an employee of your company. Please tell us why you were there."

"I went there to ski, of course. I also talked with Lisa the first day to make sure the photo shoot would go smoothly. We flew together in my company's private jet. She informed me that everything was all arranged and working well. My wife called to let me know she couldn't come to the lodge because the oldest teenage child was dropped off at their friend's house later than planned. Flying is no problem. She doesn't like to drive in the dark on these roads. I told her to stay home. Therefore, I made my arrangements to play cards with some friends. I do have their names and phone numbers so that you detectives can ask them. He handed his list to Doug."

"The last time you saw Lisa, she was alive. Did you see Ali Zarin?"

"No, I did not. We spent enough time together doing the golf tournament. She needed to have her holiday in Aspen. I needed my own time. She knew we wanted the photo shoot completed."

"You and Ms. Givens arranged the photo shoot."

"Yes, we did. You have your information from Ben. His statements created an uproar with the news media. I didn't appreciate the release to the press. I've already asked my lawyer if I can sue the police. He hasn't gotten back to me."

Detective Moon looked at Doug. Doug spilled his coffee on his tie. Mr. Fleming jumped up to get the napkins. There were no napkins, and Mr. Fleming left the room to find some when his administrative assistant didn't arrive.

Doug picked a new cup from the counter and poured Mr. Fleming's coffee inside. The cup Mr. Fleming used was bagged for DNA testing and dropped into Candace's purse. Mr. Fleming returned with the napkins and the interview continued.

"Mr. Fleming, we saw the news coverage and there were some angry reporter questions. One question we have is do you know where Ali Zarin is located? We're hoping that she contacted her boss. Your company would be a natural for Ali to turn for help. If so, we would like to speak with her about what happened."

Mr. Fleming relaxed. He didn't know where his other employee was located. He expressed concern for her whereabouts. He wanted to also talk with her.

"Are you familiar with a man named Latin Dooley? Lisa may have mentioned him."

"Never heard of the man. Is he a suspect?"

"Not at the present time. Do you own a gun with a silencer?"

"How dare you ask me this question. I own some guns, but not a silencer. Good heavens. Do I need to contact my lawyer before we proceed? Wasn't Lisa killed with a silencer? There are all kinds of people in this office that own guns. Ben Blake is an expert marksman. I've seen his trophies one time when I needed to drop off a signed contract. I don't think he wanted me to see his den. His friend accidentally put me in the room until he finished mowing."

"Ben never mentioned his marksman aptitude. His lack of divulging this fact seems odd. How long did Ben Blake work for your company?"

Mr. Fleming hesitated. "Human Resources would know the answer, but I believe around twelve to fifteen years. My wife received his resume from someone. I don't recall the name."

Detective Moon frowned. "You may want to contact your lawyer after I ask the next question. Did you or your company know that Lisa was three months pregnant?"

The interviewed man caved. "I might have known. I can't remember if she told me or not. She said something about a doctor appointment. I don't usually pay any attention to my employees taking time off. Are you absolutely certain?"

"Yes, the autopsy report revealed those sad facts."

"The news media doesn't know yet?"

"No. I'm not sure how much longer we can keep this information from the public. We expect you will keep this news private."

"I respectfully will do so. Are we through talking now?"

"Is there anyone you can think of who would want Lisa or Ali dead? This would be inside and outside your organization?"

"No. Our employees have their competitive difficulties, but there's no one that comes to mind. We do our jobs and go home to our families. Lisa had

118

difficulty at first with Ali's promotion. She knew her in college, you know. She recommended the raven. Lisa told me Ali loved the bird. I hear Ali tossed the bird. The director told me when he left a message on my phone after the shoot was over."

"Why do you think Lisa lied to you?"

Mr. Fleming shook his head. "I wish I knew. It's too late to confront her."

"Did your wife like Lisa and Ali?"

"I don't understand the question. My wife knows the two women. They weren't friends. My wife moves in different circles."

Detective Moon made a motion to Doug who turned off the recorder. Doug left the room.

"Could Lisa's baby have been your unborn child?"

Gene Fleming got up from his chair and went to the window.

"Anything is possible. We did have a brief flirtation about three months ago. She also was seeing someone else."

"Did she ever mention the name of the person she was dating?"

"Not that I can recall. Again, there was no reason to talk about her love life or mine. We're both independent people."

"If you think of anything that would help us, please give me a call." Detective Moon handed him her card. He put the card in his pocket without looking at it.

She knew he would never call the police. Their conversation was over.

## 15 Sheriff Cray's Call

**Sheriff Cray was** one of those people who loved to read old case files while he was in the office bored out of his mind by no prisoners in his cell block. During his search in police files, he ran across an item that led to another item, and so on.

He scratched his head.

"I don't believe what is there in front of me. I wonder if Detective Moon has found this little gem."

He yelled for his receptionist to get that Candace woman's cell phone number for him. The receptionist hurriedly pulled up the number. He dialed and left a message. Within the hour, she called him back.

"Sheriff Cray. You called me. What's up? Is your neighbor still in the area?"

"You mean, Grant Evans?"

"Yes. He's the only person we've discussed. Or has he gone back to New York?"

"No, he and his brother are still around. My understanding is that Grant is looking at some land here in New Mexico. The owner may or may not sell to the Evans. The property is a pretty piece, lots of water, and a good value for future investment."

"We see Grant owns another property. There's a new cabin on the piece. The land was purchased a few years back. Isn't the cabin and ranch enough to keep him busy? Of course, he also finds time for his lawyer job in New York. He sounds like an interesting fellow. I'd like to meet him if I'm ever in your neck of the woods."

Sheriff Cray paused for a second. "Sure, we can meet with him. Grant makes the best coffee. He flies the beans in from god knows where. Boxes of strange vegetables and fruit come in the mail every day. The postman has complained about the weight of the boxes."

Candace laughed.

"The coffee sounds fun. Why did you call me?"

He proceeded to give her the file record number that he was reviewing. It took her five minutes to access the data.

"Candace, I've got to go. There's a trucker accident. I'll call you back."

Sheriff Cray disappeared for four hours and when he called her back, she immediately answered.

"How was the accident?"

"The trucker is still with us and the beef cows he was hauling. The trucker's tires are toast."

"That's good, Andrew, I like a thick, juicy steak, but can wait until the red stuff arrives in the supermarket."

"Maybe we should have coffee and steak when you visit."

Candace was enthralled.

"You're good, sheriff."

"Thanks a bunch. Here's the story on that case file. It's about a murder in Idaho on a ski run."

"What does this have to do with my case. It looks like they never caught the killer."

"Read the autopsy report."

"Oh, she was pregnant."

"Does this case sound a little familiar to your recent Lisa Givens case?"

"Yes, it does, but the company this person worked for is different."

"Look again at the maiden name of Mrs. Fleming."

"Her father owned the news company in Idaho that this other person worked. The Emily Lund person who was murdered was their employee."

"Mrs. Fleming is the one with the money who funded Gene Fleming's news station in California."

"I see. I'm not sure how these fit, but I will look at the files more later."

"You do that. If you need my help, I'm here."

"Thank you, Sheriff Cray."

"You're welcome."

Sheriff Cray pushed back in his chair and put his feet up on his desk.

"Today's been a good day. At least, I have her attention steered somewhere else."

His cell phone rang. He picked up and stated his full name.

"Sheriff Andrew Cray, you need to get those cowboy boots off the desk."

"Detective Moon, are you checking up on me?"

Candace was enjoying the callback.

"Yes, I apologize. I did call your office to see what you were doing. The receptionist told me about your boots. They are blue and tan to match your uniform. I hope you don't mind. Receptionists like female cops. I could be in trouble with your office. I've had people tell me to mind my own business."

Sheriff Cray laughed. She distracted him as well.

"Touché."

"Yes. I'll talk to you, soon, Sheriff Cray. Have a good evening."

"Will do. You do the same."

Candace enjoyed the talk with a fellow officer. "Signing out now."

"Ditto that."

"I want you to know I'm going home. I'll send you pics of me because my police photo is terrible."

Sheriff Cray almost fell out of his chair. The detective sent him photos of her hair. On one side were two bobby pins with hands. On the other side was a bobby pin with a gun.

He texted Detective Moon back, "Hands up?"

"Correct, you win the office lottery game. Everyone pitched in to buy a new rifle cover as the prize. The gun cover is tan and will match your boots. I'll have my receptionist mail the box to your office. Oh, tell your wife that I see from the old record file that you are definitely working too hard."

The sheriff laughed. "Doesn't she already know this piece of information. Thank you for the box. I'll talk to you soon."

"Roger, and out."

Sheriff Cray stayed in his office thinking about his next move. He needed to talk to Grant. He was trying to think up an excuse to drive to their cabin. Currently, he couldn't think of a reason. He would have to go home and think harder. He didn't want to make Grant an enemy. He thought of the two boys as his sons. His wife could only produce females. He didn't know that his sperm was to blame.

He arrived home and his wife saved some hot, spicy tacos for him.

"God loves a sweet woman who makes tacos and I'm lucky."

Sheriff Cray heated up the meat and crunched on the tacos. The lettuce and cheese oozed out on his plate. He dug in the kitchen drawer for a fork. Helping himself to two more tacos, he knew that the antacid jar was in the bathroom. He put his plate in the kitchen sink and the pans filled with soapy water.

Sheriff Cray crawled in bed and wondered where Ali Zarin was tonight. He hoped she was safe. He hoped she was with Grant.

## 16 Pinyon Proposal & Hitch

**Grant ran the** machine which rolled the helicopter on a platform to the launch area. Ali waited excitedly inside the storage facility until he motioned for her to enter the helicopter. He shut the door for her, walked around to the pilot's side, and crawled in. He put his headphones on and motioned for her to do the same. The engine started and the blades turned.

Carefully, the helicopter lifted off the pad and he flew toward the horizon. Grant talked in his microphone as they toured the boundaries of the cabin land. He pointed out landmarks on the property, an old rundown building, a large stand of trees, and an emergency phone.

He explained the land line was already there when he bought the property. The phone company inspected the line and put the phone back in use. They replaced the old one with a newer style phone. Grant wanted the emergency phone because sometimes the cell service wasn't there. The phone was an additional measure of safety.

Ali was pleased with their tour. He pointed out the road they traveled when they arrived and the other road which led to the main highway. After their tour, he flew back to the launch pad and their plan was pizza at the cabin.

Grant knew that Ali was impressed with his third property. She saw his condo in New York once. There wasn't anything she didn't know about Grant. He shared his world with her and his friends.

The helicopter landed and Ali went to the cabin to make the pizza dough. Grant would finish storing the machine and tend to their horses. He went to the cabin and sat down to hot pizza filled with hamburger, mushrooms, and black olives. Grabbing several large pieces, he ate two slices before speaking.

"I have this friend and his wife. They live about a half hour away near the highway in a large ranch home built into the hills. He is a registered magistrate and can perform ceremonies."

Ali stopped eating her pizza. Their past three and a half weeks together were fun. They'd gotten close again. She knew that he must return to his lawyer job.

"What are you trying to ask me?"

"I think you know the answer. My feelings about us have never changed. Everyone in this state knows that I'm in love with you. You are who I want to love. You've been the only one my heart has wanted for a long time. You are sexy and funny without trying. My body's passion belongs to only you. There, I've told you too much. I just need to add this is not a game. I'm very serious. Together we'll be amazing."

"Everyone?"

Grant ate the last bite, laughed, and knew his plea for marriage needed to be upped a little higher. He got down on his knees.

"Marry me. I promise to be a good husband."

"And faithful?" teased Ali.

Grant shook his head. She always was a difficult woman. Then it dawned on him. Ali Zarin accepted his proposal. He kissed her hands.

"Faithful is my name if you think that I'm your world and have said yes."

Ali thought of a better answer. "I can be your world, too. I've never been the same since we met. There, we've both said too much. We are on equal playing ground. I love you but we'll need to wait until I can get a white dress."

Grant kissed her on the lips. There wasn't going to be any delay. There always was a way to move obstacles. "We'll get you a white dress, veil, nightie, slippers. Overnight mail is no problem. Now can we get to more kisses?"

Ali wet her lips to drive Grant a little crazier. "How do we do this? My name will be on record."

Grant saw the gleam of fun in Ali's eyes. "We'll ask my friend to hold off on mailing the marriage license application. We can do the ceremony and sign our names to the document. We will sort of be legal."

"I can do kind of or sort of. What about a ring?"

Grant thanked his lucky stars he was prepared. He disappeared and came back with a blue box. Ali was amazed he purchased a ring.

"How long have you hidden this ring?"

"I was in New York feeling lonely and blue. I saw the blue boxes in the jewelry store window and went inside. I wasn't in there very long. I knew your size and they showed me this perfect ring. I bought the ring after the cabin was built. The wedding band was sent later. I've brought the rings here waiting for the perfect moment."

"This cabin is different from the ranch, why?"

Grant sighed. He would need to explain. "I tried to build the cabin to match your taste. I needed to impress you when I asked you to come for a visit."

"You were going to get in contact with me?"

"Yes, we'd been apart too long. If the cabin didn't work, I planned to move to Los Angeles."

Grant embraced Ali. She was smiling sweetly. He told her what she wanted to hear.

"You are crazy, Grant."

"Come on. You get the dress ordered. I'll make the arrangement with my friend for flowers and cake. There's champagne in the wine refrigerator. We can crockpot a chicken and do rice. We'll have a great party. My friend, Red Drake and his wife, Lara, will be our witnesses. We'll get them to take pictures."

"What are you going to wear and what about your ring?"

"I have a few wool suit jackets and slacks here. Also dress shirts. My dad's old ring fits and will do fine until we can select one. The ring is silver with small diamonds. I'm covered. Are you happy now?"

"Perfectly. I'm glad things came together. I'm pleased you were coming to find me. I think we can work out the small stuff."

"I know that we can."

Grant kissed Ali more tenderly than before. Her eyes were burning brighter. Another kiss would seal the deal. He knew his next question would get her caught off guard. He was willing to risk a back step. There were plans to make with Ali beyond a wedding.

"How many kids do you want? We could get started right away."

Ali couldn't believe him.

"Whoa, too fast, Grant. You need to do a full stop. We need to slow down. No thinking babies until after the killer is caught. However, we can practice and work toward our dream life."

"First, we take care of marriage business."

They both went into the den. She let him help her pick a white lace, fitted dress. It was all right for him to see the dress. He would see the dress in a day or two at their marriage. She was sure there wasn't any more bad luck coming their way.

The dress arrived and the two lovers were married. Ali liked his friends. They arrived in Indian ceremonial dress. The reception dinner was perfectly cooked. Red brought jalapeno peppers and cream cheese which they stuffed, rolled in eggs, dipped in bread crumbs, and broiled. Lara made a homemade, triple layer, carrot cake with white buttercream frosting. Yellow flowers adorned the top.

Wildflowers from Lara's garden were Ali's bouquet. Pictures were taken and documents were signed. Ali's lace dress shown against Grant's navy-blue blazer and slacks. They looked every bit the handsome couple. Grant's arms protectively touched her waist. She could barely move without Grant holding her hand. He was filled with excitement about their future.

The photo and article would appear in the local paper after their wedding license application was approved. Lara gave Ali a beautiful turquoise and silver necklace. A silver buckle was given to Grant which was made by his friend. The two men shook hands and hugged each other.

Grant's brother, Milan, was called before the ceremony. They didn't want to leave him out, but knew he was busy taking care of the ranch, and he was watching the sheriff's vehicle monitor their ranch road from a distance.

Their two friends left the cabin, taking home cake in a foil wrapper for their kids.

The married couple jumped on the bed before falling into each other's arms. Later, they fell sound asleep after Grant checked the horses and security cameras.

A fire kept their room extra warm. Clothes were not required when their bodies touched. They were alone in their mountaintop retreat. A lifetime with Ali would be too short for Grant's liking. He thought briefly about the raven. He wondered if they could float back and forth between worlds. In case, he couldn't, Grant was going to make use of every moment for the rest of his life.

"What are you thinking so deeply, Grant?"

"I was thinking about sunlight, pleasure, and a lifetime of loving. I'm crazy about you."

Ali said, "A lifetime of loving sounds perfect. The air is sweet and the sunlight beautiful. We'll be crazy beautiful."

Grant couldn't be more pleased.

## 17 Another Murder

**Detectives Moon and** Constantine looked at the grim scene. There was blood all over the young man's apartment.

Candace read the suicide note on the table. She didn't believe the words written. There was a feeling in the air that was wrong. Doug bagged the note.

The coroner arrived and declared the man as definite dead body. The coroner's van took the body away for an autopsy. The detectives watched while the police continued with their pictures. There was drug paraphernalia on the nightstand in the bedroom. The man was in his pajamas and the television was blaring. Doug put gloves on and turned the machine off.

Candace noted the takeout dinner containers in the trash. A bottle of vodka and glass were on the kitchen table.

"The scene looks like the man ate a nice dinner, fixed a drink, and was going to get high before going to bed. I believe he was next interrupted by a knock on the door. I think he knew the person and let the perpetrator into his sweet den. He probably offered him part of his drug package or at least a drink. The cupboard door is ajar where the drink glasses reside. Then the man takes this fancy knife out of his briefcase and attacks his friend."

"There weren't too many cuts. The killer knew exactly where to carve to cause huge blood flow," said Doug.

Candace bent over the knife. "Does this knife look like part of a set. Somehow, the knife looks familiar. I wonder if the knife was used before. Have the lab check the knife thoroughly. Let's see what they find."

"Do you remember the taxidermist's house?"

"Yes, I'm thinking the same thing. We might have a match to the knife set. Let's hope Latin doesn't run before we can get the search warrant."

"There's already a media van out front. A neighbor or the landlord may have contacted them," said Doug.

Candace looked outside and saw the van.

"They might have been driving through the neighborhood hoping to catch Ali's boyfriend with some dirt."

"Do you think Ali Zarin might show herself now that her boyfriend, Rad Newman, is dead?"

"Let's hope she stays put. I don't like the looks of this new murder. We have a killer and a second body. I don't believe Ali killed Lisa Givens. My gut says there is maybe more than one person involved. Latin knows something or did this. This murder also tells me the boyfriend knew something, saw something, or was involved. Players can turn on each other. Remember Hamlet."

Doug vaguely remembered the play. He didn't want to admit to Candace he wasn't into the arts.

"We might see more players fall. They've all protested too much."

Doug said, "They pretended to be friends and were the opposite?"

"Exactly."

Detective Moon talked with the local police and finally, the two detectives left the scene. They ran to their car to avoid the news reporters.

"It was hard for people to know their enemies a couple centuries ago and even harder today. People are more skilled with their disguises. This will delay our investigation further. The killer is trying to deflate our ideas or steer us into another direction."

Doug was tired. He thought they could go on vacation by now.

"Consider me shaken."

Candace nodded. She thought about the file Sheriff Cray mentioned. She put the file aside. Perhaps she needed to dig deeper. She was not about to give up on solving this case. But the pressure would come from her boss to find Ali Zarin. She had a hunch where she could find the woman.

Detective Candace Moon called Grant Evans ranch and found out Grant returned to New York City. His review of Mr. Johnson's proposal was over, and he would continue with his job as lawyer to a large firm. Candace wasn't too keen on traveling to New York City.

With the boyfriend's death occurring, there was a reason for the trip. She wondered if Grant Evans would be delighted about the boyfriend. She hoped he would have a good alibi. She wasn't sure about Ali's feelings. The woman should have made contact by now with the old boyfriend.

"Unless, there's another boyfriend on the scene. Grant Evans seemed a likely prospect. He was both handsome and rich."

Candace said, "He's my choice for Ali. Distance will or will not make the heart stronger. Plus, there's the other woman, Alessandria Morgan. She talked to a news reporter about Grant Evans and his relationship to Ali Zarin. I'm not pleased that the Albuquerque Newspaper has his name in large print. I wish this Alessandria called us first. The article could alert our killer to do his research on the man."

Doug pushed his hair out of the way. There wasn't time to get a haircut with the heavy involvement on the case.

"I wonder if Grant knew Alessandria's intentions?"

"I'll bet you a box of donuts that he didn't know," said Candace.

"No, you don't. I'll bet you a dinner he didn't know."

"Doug, I like the way you gamble."

Detective Moon's next step would be the arrest of Latin Dooley. The interview with Grant Evans would need to wait for a future time.

## 18 Latin's Arrest

**The police cars** surrounded the house of Latin Dooley. The police knocked on the door with the search warrant in their hands. Detectives Moon and Constantine saw the little man ushered into a police car. The little man was complaining all the way out of his house. He was worried about his equipment and stuffed birds.

Candace looked at Doug. "We'll wait until the police process him and his house. We can check into our motel rooms and grab an early dinner."

"I'm really hungry. There was a nice-looking burger place across from the motel. They even have a website."

Doug reviewed the menu.

"Oh, boy, triple bacon cheeseburger with garlic fries is the special tonight. Oh, darn the special doesn't start until five o'clock. We do have time to check in first."

"Did you see any salads on their menu?"

"There is a Mexican basket or California salad with avocados."

"Avocados aren't in season. They must use the jarred stuff. I'm not sure I can eat another fiery hot batch of beans."

Doug scrolled down the menu. "You're in luck, they have chicken fingers with mustard sauce."

"Perfect."

When they were finished with their meal, the detectives drove to the local jail. A sullen Latin was brought to the interview room in his prison garb."

"I didn't do nothing."

"Anything. You say you didn't do anything."

"That's what I said, nothing."

"There is a knife missing from your original collection. We see that you tried to trick us by purchasing a replacement knife. The replacement is in your collection. Your real knife was used to kill a young man named, Rad Newman. You remember him. He was Ali Zarin's boyfriend."

"He was murdered with a knife, big deal. Lots of people get murdered with sharp instruments. I'm assuming the knife was sharp. I keep mine sharp. Most taxidermists like this style of knives. I didn't know the man, Brad or did you say Rad? My mind gets confused. I didn't get anything good to eat. They gave me onion soup and purple jelly with my crackers. Who eats that crap? When did you say he was murdered?"

"Two days ago."

"I was home with my birds."

"Were there any living things there to verify your alibi? Possibly your neighbors saw you outside."

"My neighbors shrink when they see me because I know they called the law. They blame me for the snake on their property. I only moved a few dead mice. I didn't know the mice traps were across the property line. The only living thing that saw me was the snake. The stupid thing came back and is in my garage. I still can't put my van inside."

Doug took over the interview. "A snake doesn't count. Why did you kill Mr. Newman? Was he going to tell us some valuable information?"

"My knife was stolen. Lisa Givens took my knife to hurt Ali Zarin. Lisa told me that was why she couldn't give my knife back. She told me this in Aspen at the rental. I didn't believe she would use my knife."

Candace said, "Per your first written statement, you told us that you never talked to Lisa or Ali. Now you're telling me you talked with Lisa about your knife at their rental?"

Latin looked sideways, "I told you I forget things. I talked with her. Maybe it was the lodge or outside the lodge. She had several bags of luggage when she checked in. I saw them in her car. I wondered why she needed so many bags. She must have hidden my knife in one of those bags. You should look for the bag. She would need to have wrapped the knife in heavy plastic. Maybe she put the knife in her large makeup bag."

"Did you see Lisa's makeup bag?"

"No, no, I'm just speculating. She wore lots of eye shadow."

Candace pushed back from the table. She worried the knife could have been used to hurt Ali and that was why they couldn't find her. Candace hated the little man for lying to them initially.

"She took my handkerchief, too. Lisa was a thief that I let into my home. Now she's trying to frame me."

"Your fingerprints were all over the knife. There's nothing we can do for you."

Latin looked scared.

"I touch my knives on occasion. That's why there's fingerprints. I can do a deal with you. I've heard things. The boyfriend and Lisa were plotting to hurt Ali."

Doug shook his head. "You're like a rat in a hole trying to find a way out. You're making things up."

"No, I overheard her talking in the lodge. I hid behind a planter."

"Did you see Mr. Newman?"

"Not exactly. Lisa was with a man. I presumed the man was Newman. He wore a hat and I couldn't see his face."

Candace shook her head. "You may have heard Lisa and Newman's nemesis or adversary. You could be in trouble."

The two detectives left the room and Latin was escorted back to his cell. He didn't know the word, so he asked the guard. The guard told him, "Enemy or rival." Latin's face fell.

Latin heard the raven from the photo shoot laughing at him, and the bird's head was bobbing up and down. Latin wondered if he was going crazy. Lately, he couldn't find his glasses. He wondered if he could get new glasses while he waited in jail. Latin forgot about his circumstance and worried about the glasses.

"Is there going to be a late-night snack at the jail," asked Latin.

"The food service people went home."

"You got any mints in your pocket?"

The guard unlocked the prison cell.

"Guess not."

Latin's car and garage were forgotten until the next day. The snake was no longer being bothered by a taxidermist. Latin buried a metal box in his garage when the snake was gone. He didn't tell anyone about the secret box.

Latin believed that he played the scene with the detectives just right. They would remember his words. The words wouldn't matter. He knew he was smarter. The money would wait. The only thing he didn't know was who planted the knife?

## 19 Arrival of Matlock

Grant watched the news and became worried about Ali alone at the cabin in New Mexico. She was there for two weeks after he left and was doing well. Lara brought her some watercolor paper, paints, and brushes to keep Ali busy. The two women were exchanging their knowledge of the paint medium. He would be pleased to see the miniature paintings. His friend, Red, was making the frames for them out of old pinyon wood.

Luckily, the garage door people called and were ready to deliver a new insulated, special-build door for the helicopter area. He contacted Milan and asked him to stay the next two weeks while the door was installed. He told Milan to be extra alert due to the recent news about Ali's old boyfriend. Grant couldn't get away from New York.

Milan loaded the four horses and called one of the cattle hands that he knew who was available to work the ranch while he was away. Matlock arrived with his small travel trailer, parked by the ranch casita, and proceeded to get his charcoal barbeque ready.

Matlock's roller patio screen was rolled out and zippered to the trailer frame to keep the flies out. An old wool Indian rug was next laid on the blue tarp in the screened area and a lounge chair with small table finished the final scene of a man cave.

By the time Milan came back to the casita from watering and feeding the cows, Matlock was asleep in his chair. Milan fed the horses and checked their water.

Then he entered the zipper door of Matlock's porch. He kicked Matlock's boots.

The elderly cattleman stirred.

"Your charcoal is a nice ash gray. I brought you a fresh steak and baked potato. I'm going to hit the sack because I'm leaving around five o'clock."

Milan didn't need to give him any directions. Matlock knew the layout of the ranch and was familiar with the routine.

"Thanks, man for the steak. Yours are always thick and tasty. I picked up some butter in town and eggs. I should be all right for the duration. I'll probably eat a late lunch at Rosie's in case you return during the day. I hear she has a bunch of pups from her sheep dog. I'm going to look at the crew while I'm in town.

"If there's any trouble, be sure to contact the sheriff straight away. Grant doesn't like trespassers."

"There's nothing worse than varmits and trespassers. I say shoot em dead."

"I think Grant would prefer that you ask them nicely to get off his land."

"Well, that would sure spoil a man's day. I really liked the old days better when a man put notches on his gun. Anyway, I've got my revolver handy. She's loaded and ready. No sir, there ain't nobody getting the jump on me.

Milan laughed. "How come I got the jump on you? Your eyes were closed, and you were snoring."

"I heard your footsteps and my eyes were slits. I can appear to be sleeping to outsiders."

"Didn't you tell me last year that you traded a buffalo hide for some hearing aids?"

Matlock touched his hair. "See they are in and working just fine. I also brought some traps to hide under my rug, just in case. That is until I get a new dog. Don't step on the green bird on the rug."

Milan saw the green figure on the rug. It was hard to tell the shape.

"I know. The bird used to be a bright blue. My old Betsy dog died. Bless her gypsy heart, she liked to pee on that spot. Now the bird's green. The dog was a major protector. She knew an evil person's walk. She growled different."

Milan wasn't about to touch the rug spot.

Matlock walked out the makeup porch screen. He threw both the steak and potato on the grill. First, he wrapped the potato in foil with a half stick of butter. He bought the salted butter stuff. There was no use wasting your own private salt shaker when some other company could pack the butter-thing better. He'd eat whichever one was done first. He was glad there were no chives in the area. He hated onions and chives. His motto was, *Let the trespassers steal em.* More than likely, the potato and butter would be the winner. His steaks were usually cooked well done with a crispy burn on the fat.

Milan went to his casita and was glad he closed his windows earlier. The air conditioner made the place cool and free of burned grease smell.

In the morning, Milan heard music coming from the trailer of Matlock. He recognized the song as a shepherd's chant, an opera song sung by a famous female artist. Milan was impressed. He was moved. He

144

once saw the female artist with Grant in New York City. It was a one-time Grant move to bring culture to his brother's life. The music resonated in his brother's sole, unknown to Grant. Milan was pleased by the song on this morning and future possibilities. The song reminded him of his mother. Grant told him his mother loved opera. That's what made Milan listen and research the songs his mother loved. He bought several CD's.

The horses and gear were loaded by Milan. He was humming the aria. The ranch and casita were locked. He threw the bunch of Albuquerque Newspapers onto the table in the foyer. He didn't read them much. The paper was good for starting a fire outside.

On second thought, Milan grabbed a couple newspapers and left them near Matlock's trailer. Matlock loved to read. After the words were read, he folded the newspapers into fans and used them to swat the flies. Once the paper got dirty, then he threw them in the fire. Resourceful was Matlock's name.

It was time for the horse trailer to roll. However, the gas light came on and Milan would need to stop in town to get gas. Milan was afraid his planning-ahead skills were a might off. The sheriff was walking out with a steaming cup of coffee. He strolled over to Milan's rig.

"Out of gas again? They need to put a beeper on the dial for boys like you. I guess a beeper wouldn't be heard when you've got the radio blaring."

Milan looked at the sheriff crosswise. He wasn't in the mood.

"I know, it's none of my business when you buy gas. Where in the world are you going so early in the morning?"

Milan sighed. He wished he could go inside and get a hot dog, chips, and cola for breakfast. The food would have to wait.

Milan explained the insulated door arrived and Grant wanted him to supervise the work. He told the sheriff he should be gone two weeks, and Matlock was watching their animals. He told the sheriff about the green bird and what was under the rug.

"I appreciate the update and it's nice to see Matlock hasn't changed. I bet he still burns his steak."

"And eats his potato skins with butter. The hay feeder for the cows arrived at the ranch this week except I was having difficulty putting the device together. I decided not to have Matlock work the plan. The device is circular and I'm sure he would make the metal an S-shape. We can't have a screwup job on the feeder. Grant would blame me."

"I know how particular Grant can be about a door. I'm glad he decided to get those Steadman brothers to build a new door. I've seen their work. When you get back, I'll help you with the feeder if Grant isn't here. That's funny about the S-shape. My wife will be pleased about Matlock being in the area. She'll make him some pork tamales for sure. I'll have to deliver them to Mr. Matlock and listen to his silence. He couldn't figure out why my wife was still living with me. We argued about the better places she could live. One night we played cards and came to an agreement or understanding."

"What was the agreement?"

"Tahiti."

"Tahiti is where your wife wants to live?"

"Heck, no, it's where I said I'd take her for vacation next year. Matlock can't argue with me about my wife for that long. Does he still have the dog?"

"No, but he's going to look at Rosie's pups."

The radio went off in the sheriff's vehicle. "I've got to run."

After filling the tank Milan went inside the gas station store, bought breakfast, and drove to the cabin. When he arrived, he noted Ali had been crying.

"Do you want to talk about your boyfriend? I'm a good listener."

Ali could see Milan was tired.

"No, I got off the phone with Grant. He assured me they caught his killer. I'm not so sure. Latin was destructive but murdering a human has consequences. He mainly stuck to birds. I'm glad to have company for two weeks. I won't become a hermit anytime soon."

"I brought the roan horse. When I was loading the first two horses, he wouldn't stop talking to me."

"I'm glad you brought him. His coat makes a pretty splash of color in the landscape. I also can try painting him and his regal nose."

Ali showed him the five framed watercolor pictures. He was pleased she put the pinyon trees in each one and signed with her married name.

"Did you know Lara has a daughter from her first marriage. She's visiting them. You might want to stop in for a visit."

"Pretty?"

"Very," said Ali.

The next two days, the new helicopter door was hung, and the Steadman brothers left. Milan went off to some local farms to look at their hay feeders. He went several times to visit Lara and Red's daughter, Laila.

In the evenings, he helped cook and do dishes. Time went by quickly. Matlock called and was ready to move to his next work gig. Milan was forced to return to the ranch and leave Ali alone. He gave the ranch address to his new friend, Laila. Milan told Ali that the daughter was very nice. Ali was pleased. A little matchmaking never hurt.

She assured Grant that she was fine. Ali didn't want to tell him she was afraid again. The nights were long and hard. She heard strange noises in the night and her nightmares started. She kept trying to see the killer's face. She wanted and didn't want to see the face. Ali put a few rifles in strategic spots in the helicopter area. She used the garage door clickers that Milan left on top of the refrigerator for Grant's return.

Arrangements were made for Lara or Red to check with Ali every other day. On occasion, they would bring her more supplies.

Milan arrived home. When Milan looked at the back field at the ranch, the hay feeder was put together and a round bale of hay was sitting in the center where the bale was supposed to reside. There a note attached.

# LINDA MCKOWN

*Missing two extra-long, heavy bolts for the unwind bar. The manufacturer is mailing to the ranch. You owe me one hundred fifty bucks more for my time. You'll have to ask the sheriff how much you owe him. Your garbage cans are full. Better dump soon or there'll be varmits. They won't eat the glass bottles, though. Better varmits than trespassers any day. My new dog's a female. I called her Birdie cause she's white and yellow. I saw a finch once. M.*

Milan was pleased until he saw the greasy, used charcoal, left in the garden. There were burnt corn husks and lime rinds in the mess. He went to get a shovel to bury the stuff. He wondered if charcoal was good for the soil.

"Probably not."

Off to the right of the mess, hanging on the wooden pole, was a leather pouch. Milan opened the strings and saw copper and silver-gray pennies inside. There was a note.

*Give the pouch and pennies to Rosie. She gets the old coins for my new pup. I finally found the pouch buried in the bottom of my toolbox. I wondered why the darn thing was so heavy. She's dating a coin dealer. Thanks. M.*

Milan went into the casita and made a call to Laila. He wanted to hear her voice. She was the most part of normal that he'd met in the last month or two. She was studying agriculture and wanted to own her own ranch someday. Milan thought some of old man Johnson's land would work nicely. He was happy and was whistling when he dropped off a nice check at the post office and the sheriff's office.

Sheriff Cray was pleased with the amount and note. He laughed when Milan stated in the note the payment was for personal services rendered and was in no way a bribe.

The work of figuring out the schematics of the hay feeder with Matlock was a fun experience. The two older men thought some idiot at the plant stole the bolts for a homemade trailer the clerk was working. They appeared to be real expensive bolts and well-made. They weren't the Chinese junk some of the cheaper hay feeders contained. They even looked at the box to make sure the item was stamped *Made in the USA*.

The special part of the two older men's friendship was eating the tamales on the grill with Mexican beer and limes.

Both men read the Albuquerque Newspaper article that Alessandria Morgan gave to the reporter. Neither men were overly impressed. Ms. Morgan wasn't considered good enough for Grant. They burned the paper when they ate the tamales.

## 20 New York City Visit

**The guard buzzed** Grant Evan's condominium to let him know two visitors arrived. He waited patiently for the knock on his door.

The city lights and sky were spectacular from his penthouse view. He put his bottle of water down and let the detectives inside.

"There is a bowl of ice and several water bottles on the marble countertop. Please help yourself. Detective Moon, you might want to use the bar towel to keep the water from dripping."

"Thank you, Mr. Evans. My partner, Doug Constantine, and I were pleased you could see us this evening. Your view of the city is amazing and as good as the view from the Empire State Building."

Grant laughed. "My building isn't quite so high. You can call me Grant during your interview. Let's sit down by the sofa."

Candace sat down on the plush gold leather. She noticed the rest of the modern furniture. The look was designer quality.

"The condominium is nicely decorated. I like the muted blue walls and white marble fireplace. The color seems to enhance the sky. Then there's the large picture of Central Park. I feel lost in the green trees."

"Thank you. A designer friend of mine helped with some of the input on wall color. She wanted to re-decorate the rooms. I didn't have the time and found the artist painting at a gallery in Greenwich Village. Besides, I like the simplicity and the view is priceless."

"I appreciate a fine artist. He's a photographer who wraps his images to a large size. I have a photo of the London Bridge in my bedroom."

"I'm familiar with his bridge images. You selected a good one."

Doug felt a little outside the conversation. He never saw Candace's bedroom.

Candace looked away from the photograph on the wall. "We aren't here to socialize with you. We do have some delicate questions to ask. The police are aware of your relationship with a suspect in a murder investigation."

Grant stiffened at the thought of Ali as a potential suspect.

"We would like to know if you know where Ali Zarin is residing? We believe she might still be alive. My team needs to talk with her regarding the Lisa Givens investigation. We have her goggles with Lisa's blood. Those black goggles seem to point us in her direction. I haven't given up the fact there is a different avenue for us to chase. Still, a killer is on the loose."

Grant looked at the fire and took the remote. He lit the fireplace.

"I appreciate your telling me your thoughts on the investigation. I'm sorry that I can't help you. Ali Zarin and I split several years ago. I've been busy with my ranch and work here. As a matter of fact, here's a picture of our sheriff with a good friend, Matlock, at my ranch. They put together a hay feeder for me."

Candace looked at the picture on the cell phone.

She knew which one in the photo was the sheriff by his gun holster and mustache. He looked just like his picture. Suddenly, she remembered that she hadn't read the old case file he sent her. Candace made a mental note to read the entire file in the future.

Grant decided to divulge some information. His hope was to steer the detectives away from Ali.

"I'm going back to my ranch soon. I've heard from Mr. Johnson. He owns a five-hundred-acre piece of land that would improve my ranch in the numbers game. The land abuts mine. I could steer my cows to his grasslands in the summer which are fed by an important stream. This would save me money in feed and hay."

Doug piped up, "I once was a ranch hand and helped drive cows or rather steer. The work was hard, and I hated the flies."

Detective Moon looked at Doug in surprise.

Grant knew the perfect answer. "A good cowboy knows how to shoot the flies. I'm amazed no one showed you how. I assume you carried a gun to scare off the wolves. They follow sheep and steer."

"No, they didn't show me."

Candace almost laughed.

"Good story, Grant. We do believe you about Mr. Johnson. We hear an oil firm has approached him."

Grant was suddenly alert, "Which oil firm?"

Candace would need to explain.

"Your Sheriff Cray alerted us to the fact that you were interested in land owned by a Mr. Johnson. I found the listing and called the realtor. He was very vocal about potential buyers for the property. He confirmed that you were interested and slipped the other company's name."

"I see. You do research all items in front of the investigation. I'm one of those items."

"Yes, you are high on our list."

Grant wasn't in the least bit surprised.

"Sheriff Cray shouldn't have told you about my future business or my relationship with Ali."

"The sheriff did so out of reluctance. He's worried about Ali Zarin. He told me she was a bright spot in his day at a barbeque. He wants to help. We want to help. If she does turn to you for support, we would appreciate a call. I believe she may have been injured in the attack and is frightened. If she's not involved in the murder, we can offer her police protection. I've put the name of the oil firm on the back of my card."

Candace handed Grant her business card. He looked at the back. He made a mental note of the oil firm.

She saw a brief glimpse of pain pass over Grant's face and then he caught himself. She wasn't sure if the pain was about Ali or the oil firm.

With exaggerated composure, he said, "I didn't really know any of her Los Angeles friends nor did I know Lisa Givens. I've never met Lisa. Have you tried talking to her co-workers? It seems to me they would have a lot more to tell you."

"We are working with her co-workers. No one has heard from Ali. Is there anyone you know that might have been unhappy with Ali to cause her harm? Did she ever mention a name specifically?"

"No, she didn't talk about work that much other than a special news piece she was excited about. The golf tournament was a yearly event. She looked forward to the celebrity interviews. Ali liked touching fame and the rich. Her focus was always work at the news media company. Nothing distracted her from her work. Her visits with me were brief and inconsequential. Our relationship was a brief interlude to what she really wanted."

Grant took a brief respite from the interview. A call came in and he left the room. He returned to the interview.

"I saw she received a promotion and I assumed she was happy. I once met her CEO and his wife when we went to a restaurant for dinner. The CEO seemed all right, and Ali never complained about Mr. Fleming. She liked and trusted her boss. She told me they worked many nights together preparing contracts. His wife was a little too bubbly for my taste."

"What do you mean by bubbly?"

"She seemed delighted that Ali and I were together."

"Would you say she was worried about her husband working with beautiful women?"

"Yes, Ali mentioned something was a little off between Mr. Fleming and his wife lately. She couldn't put her finger on their problem. She thought they were going through a rough patch. Mrs. Fleming was glad Ali was with me."

"I see. Ali's observation is interesting. I imagine she has known the couple for some time and is more in tune to office gossip."

"Ali is pretty smart and pays attention to her surroundings. That's why I was surprised to hear about her disappearance. Thank you for the oil company's name. The sheriff is a good friend. I'll talk with Mr. Johnson again about the land."

"I'm glad we could help. We have no more questions about Ali Zarin. There is one item that we should mention. You have a friend named, Alessandria Morgan, correct?"

Apprehension crossed Grant's face.

"What is there about Ms. Morgan?"

"We're sorry. Detective Constantine and I thought you would have seen the article in the Albuquerque Newspaper."

"What article?"

Candace looked at Doug.

"Alessandria gave an interview to a reporter about your relationship with Ali Zarin. Ms. Morgan went into quite a few details about Ali and about you. She hinted that the two of you were more than friends and hinted your ranch was a wonderful place to live."

Grant's phone rang and he excused himself into the other room again. His anger would need to wait until the detectives left.

"I'm sorry but the call was important. I was waiting for a colleague of mine to reschedule our meeting."

Doug said, "No problem."

Grant sat down.

"Let me be very clear. There is no relationship with Ms. Morgan nor has there ever been one. Ms. Morgan has contacts in the art world and design. On occasion, I pay her for those services. She might have given correct information about Ms. Zarin from my conversations or she may have made something up to get attention. I don't believe she knows Ali. They have never met that I'm aware of. Ali and I were friends, past tense. My ranch is a beautiful place to live. I go there to relax when I'm not being a lawyer. Ms. Morgan should have talked to me before going to a newspaper. I haven't read the article, but I will."

Candace knew the article was a surprise. She wasn't surprised about Grant's reaction.

"Let's hope Ms. Morgan's article doesn't bring unintended consequences."

"She already has. I no longer will be using her firm. I believe she did the article to help her newspaper friend snare an article and get Ms. Morgan's business name in the paper."

"If you think of anything or see Ali, let her know about either one of us detectives. We think she might eventually remember something."

"I'll keep your card available. Good evening, detectives."

When Candace and Doug were alone in the taxi, he told her the interview was a disappointment. He was thinking about the photograph in his partner's bedroom.

"I am pleased with our interview. Mr. Evans has the power and means to keep Ali hidden for a long time. I saw the obvious from a woman's viewpoint. The man is in love with Ali Zarin. He talked art to cover his love."

"You think she is in one of his homes?"

"Yes, most specifically his cabin in the pines. He never mentioned the property. I understand the complex is a gem in high country. With 1800 acres, the property is extensive. The cabin also wasn't in Alessandria's article. I must wonder about her reasoning. Maybe, the place is Ms. Morgan's baby. Ms. Morgan is an interior designer and buys gallery items for her clients. I bet she decorated the cabin in some of the rooms. Mr. Evans did, however, talk about the ranch near Albuquerque and let us into his New York suite."

"Mr. Evans seemed upset about the article. He will read the newspaper online. Should we ask Sheriff Cray to investigate the cabin?"

"No, not yet. The time is too soon. Ali was probably injured. A man in love would feel a woman's pain. Grant, briefly, let go of himself and showed a pained look. She's alive and probably can't remember her attacker. Speaking of attacker, there's still the killer roaming the halls, skirting our attempts to find him. We have a few more cages to rattle first. The comment about the Flemings at a restaurant was an interesting point. Ali did talk to Grant about the office."

Doug opened the taxi door for his partner and sat down inside the vehicle. He was mesmerized by his partner's ability to see and comprehend an individual's personality. He wondered what she thought of him.

"Let's get my shopping done. We'll take a brief evening at a nice Chinese restaurant before we catch the shut-eye back to LA."

Doug settled down in the taxi, relieved they wouldn't discuss the case until they reached LA. He would drift into sleep on the airplane until she talked to him. He didn't know Candace would be wide awake on the airline reading an old, open case file.

"Was Ben Blake in Aspen the day of the murder?"

Doug sat upright. "I suppose you want me to research that little human."

Candace remembered Doug's comment about stupid.

"Absolutely correct. Check the car rental agencies, too."

"Always."

## 21 Prison Visit

**The prison guard** brought Latin into the room where the bird man sat behind a glass partition.

Latin moved slowly as his feet were chained. They were chained because he tried to climb the chain link fence several times. He hid his hands which were a might sore and scarred from the electric fence.

"Hector Hansen, what brings you to this sanitary cesspool?"

"Is the place a little too clean for an old man?"

"They make me take too many baths. My skin is about to fall off. My teeth have turned two shades of white from dental cleaning. The bright orange clothes are hard on my eyes. They make me see spots that I know aren't there. Then they put us in this dusty yard where the wind blows. My pants are so filled with sand, my toilet gets plugged. There's crap everywhere. I'm handed a mop and must clean the floor. I've thought about using the mop somewhere else."

"Whoa," said Hector, "You've got to get a grip. They want the prisoners to go bonkers. If a prisoner goes bonkers, then the prison guards will have less work. The guards turn in a report. If the report is bad, the report is good for the prisoner. The psychiatrist is called on the best food day to put him in a good mood. The guards want the psychiatrist's blessing. Then the prisoners get moved to a nice mental institution."

"Are you completely nuts? Mental institution. I'm not that dumb or ill. How dare you insult my intelligence?"

160

"Listen old man, you need to calm down or the guard will put you back in your cell. Think about how nice the grounds are around a mental institution. You get to go outside and water the roses. They cook roast beef, mashed potatoes, and make gravy. The farmers donate corn on the cob to institutions. There are trees with birds. You've liked birds your whole life. There's no snakes or racoons either."

Latin was thinking about his garage. He did order black paint but didn't get an opportunity to paint. The weather turned to rain and the wood was too wet. He was going to pour the rest of the black paint with some cement to seal the snake hole. Then he thought up a better object to place next to the snake hole.

"You're right. A good, old fashioned dinner is required. The corn would be a bonus. The corn here is runny and they put crackers in the mix. You could repair the holes around my chimney with their corn mush. My health is in danger being at this facility. I should talk to my lawyer and let him know that I'm hungry and insane."

Hector shook his head. "You don't talk to the lawyer yet. First you start making a scene in the prison. You drop your lunch tray with the corn mush and start crying. Next, you scream about ghosts eating your strawberries and so on."

"I try to climb the metal fences."

"Exactly right. Give them a reason to file a report. The more things you can think of to do, the better. You make the report as bad as you can."

Latin understood, "Super bad report, check."

"What day is the best food day? We need to look at the monthly menu."

"The first Wednesday next month is pork roast with red barbeque sauce. I saw French fries on the chart. The meal listed is the only one that sounds good enough to eat. The guard told me the barbeque sauce was in a great big can. They used to make the homemade stuff until someone died."

Hector frowned. He wasn't sure if Latin was messing with him.

"You do something really bad the Thursday after the pork meal, so their report is sent Friday. The psychiatrist will be scheduled for the second Wednesday."

"You are absolutely the craziest person I know."

Hector almost touched the glass. He twirled his black onyx ring.

"Crazy isn't my name, old man. You need to keep your voice down. My plan will work. Trust me."

Latin pondered what Hector said to him.

After a few minutes, Hector told him, "I need a favor from you."

"Can't you see that I'm in a jail cell? How can I possibly do anyone a favor? Now who's the totally stoned person in the room? I could use a little marijuana. You will bring me some when we get to the mental institution."

"Be quiet, the guard will hear you. Yes, I will get the marijuana," said Hector. "And Ali Zarin. We need to find her. She could be the key to your getting out of this place."

"Ali wouldn't lift a fig to help me. I told the detectives she wouldn't see me."

Hector saw the guard motion five minutes.

"If we find her, she may, inadvertently help us. You have contacts in here that know how the police investigation is going on the Lisa Given's murder. The police will find Ali and we'll be standing in the wings."

"Hmmm. I don't know about your idea."

"My idea is worth a try. Think about it, old friend."

Latin saw the guard nod. "Old friend. I've been thinking about how bad my life got after I let you and Lisa Givens into my house. I'm re-thinking about the snake. There's more than one snake on my grounds."

"No, you're just confused. We bird people stick together. Don't let this prison cesspool get to you. While we wait for the agreed Thursday date, eat lots of oranges. Oranges contain vitamin C. Vitamin C will make you stronger. You do want to get out of here. I'm your ticket."

"Okay, okay. Don't throw my words back at me," said Latin. He would use the man, Hector. There was Latin's money and a trip waiting in his future. Hector was unimportant and a sap.

Latin scratched his waistband and the guard quickly came over to make sure the prisoner didn't have any metal objects from the noon lunch tray.

Hector watched as Latin was frisked and taken away. His plan with Latin might work.

He waved at Latin as the man was escorted from his view. Latin looked meanly at the different guard. This guard prodded his prisoner to move along.

Hector left the room and walked freely out of the prison. Latin would hate guards like he hated his neighbors. He noted how high the fence wiring was and where the guards were stationed.

Hector's other partner was pushing him for information regarding the murder investigation and the whereabouts of a co-worker. Hector's man would need to help him prepare false documents for Latin Dooley and a prison break.

## 22 DNA Test Results

**Detective Moon was** unhappy with the DNA test results. There was no match with Lisa Given's dead baby to Gene Fleming. With no match, her theories about the investigation were possibly wrong and would need to be thrown out the window.

Doug sat in their office eating a cinnamon donut. He offered Candace one and she shook her head. She went into the break room and he could hear the food machine drop a sandwich into the delivery slot.

"Egg salad again?"

"Yes, eggs are good for you. They help me think."

"They smell."

"Eggs are supposed to smell. It's because of the mustard and mayonnaise. The manufacturer uses the cheap stuff. The mayonnaise isn't real."

"Then, why do you buy egg salad?"

"Because I like the stuff more than the other sandwiches and packaged items. All you're getting is a sugar high on donuts. Next thing you know, you'll be panicking about everything."

Doug frowned. "I don't panic." He made a googly face with his fingers.

"See. Sugar makes you weird."

Doug opened a cleaning towelette and wiped the sugar off his fingers and face.

"Speaking of weird, where do we go from here? The DNA doesn't match and there goes one suspect off the list. It's a good thing we didn't turn the DNA into our boss. How do we find the father of Lisa's unborn child? We have no boyfriend attached to her from the office. There was no one at the funeral."

"Lisa might have thought Mr. Fleming was the father. Let's roll out a scenario. She's happy to be pregnant because now she's insured of a promotion. She wants to undo the photo shoot except it's too late to cancel. Mr. Fleming is her ticket to money, i.e. child support and maintenance. This wouldn't sit too well with Mrs. Fleming because the news station was built with her father's money. There might be more money out the window to hush the baby news. I doubt Lisa would consider an abortion because she's Catholic. Scenario two: Lisa knows there's a possibility Mr. Fleming isn't the father but uses the ruse anyway. The real father could be someone else. Who would Lisa want? She wants everything Ali Zarin has. Her boyfriend might be Ali's boyfriend."

Doug stands up.

Candace asks, "Where are you going?"

"I'm going to the break room to get egg salad."

Candace pounded on the table. Doug could be funny. She laid her head on the table. She was tired from reading on the airplane the night before.

Doug returned. "Tell me about the old case file you read."

"Ben Blake used to work for Mrs. Fleming's father. His name was on the employee roster. There was a young woman in the father's company that was

166

murdered a long time ago. The case was never solved. We're possibly looking for the same gun or one similar?"

Doug bit into his sandwich. He wasn't impressed. Getting up, he walked to the condiment area, grabbed several packets of hot sauce, relish, mustard, and mayonnaise. He opened the two pieces and squirted the entire packets on top of the salad.

"This is way better. Here, you should try a bite."

"No, thanks. My stomach just flipped out."

"Ben Blake working at old man Fleming's business could be a coincidence."

Candace sat up. "Yes, there is the third scenario, we have the same murderer or blackmailer. We have a lot of if's and maybe's in all three."

"How does Latin fit into the mess?"

"I think he was used or found something. The police do have him on not reporting a possible crime. The judge will keep him in prison."

Doug grinned. He didn't like the taxidermist.

"Latin gets involved because he tried to see Ali and was at the location of the murder. Latin hears Lisa talk to someone about hurting Ali. Lisa and a man are our two suspects. Only Lisa is dead. That leaves Latin and the unknown man. Ben's a third coincidence or an accomplice."

Candace grinned. The two detectives were back on the same page.

"I believe we need to interview Mrs. Fleming and Mr. Blake one more time. Do you think he will let us see his gun collection?"

Doug handed her the list of guns registered to Blake.

"No match."

"Nope, but he was in Aspen. Here's a copy of the car rental receipt."

Candace reviewed the car rental check in and out times.

"Good. Let's get a search warrant on Blake."

"I'm already typing the request." The egg sandwich has stuck in his mouth while he finished the request and hit the send button. He moved quickly for his napkin when the slime oozed out.

Candace handed Doug her napkin.

"Ben Blake has become a person of interest. Only this time, he's kicked his butt to the top of the list."

## 23 Mrs. Fleming Interview

**Mrs. Fleming was** sitting next to a tea cart when the two detectives arrived in her garden room. The tea set was brightly polished silver. The tea cart was maple wood. The whole room looked like something out of an antique store.

"I love this room. My husband can't stand the furniture. The furniture belonged to my grandfather. Gene's style is racier and more modern. Memories of my home are important and always good. Tea, detectives?"

Doug was the first to take the thin porcelain cup. He quickly sat down before the thing would break in his hands.

"Sugar or cream?"

"No, maam. I'm fine with my black oolong plain."

Candace shook her head. Doug was being overly polite until the food arrived.

A maid brought in open faced chicken salad sandwiches. Doug wondered how they got the bread slices so small. He took three sandwiches. Candace frowned at him, so he gave her one. He was surprised by a spice inside.

Candace said, "Cardamom."

"Yes, cardamom. Consuelo, you forgot the dessert."

"No, maam. I couldn't carry more than two trays. I'll go get the dessert. Excuse me."

Mrs. Fleming helped herself to one of the sandwiches, putting cucumber slices on top. Then she impatiently rang a bell. The maid quickly brought in a small tray of petit four cakes. Mrs. Fleming frowned at her maid.

Again, Doug looked at the one-inch pieces and grabbed three cakes. He didn't share with Candace.

Candace helped herself to the second dish of remaining cucumber slices. She knew she shouldn't have skipped lunch. There was no salt shaker on the tea cart. Candace saw a drawer on the tea cart and wondered if there was a salt shaker inside. The drawer front held a small key hole. Candace wondered if the drawer was locked.

Mrs. Fleming noticed Candace looking at the drawer.

"Salt. There's no salt," said Detective Moon.

Mrs. Fleming rung the bell harder for Consuelo to bring salt and pepper.

"I don't know why you want to interview me. Well, I think that I know why. You see I hired an investigative firm to follow Ali Zarin because I thought she was having an affair with my husband. I canceled the arrangement after seeing Ali with her boyfriend, Grant Evans at a restaurant."

Detective Moon looked vague.

"Was there some reason you suspected Ali of an affair?"

"Yes, Lisa Givens told me."

Now Candace was confused.

"Why would Lisa tell you such a thing?"

"Lisa was always jealous of Ali. I saw her several times make faces to Ali's back. I ignored Lisa's childish antics. Lisa didn't know I saw her displeasure. She was a good reporter. Can you imagine my surprise when Lisa later told me that she was pregnant with my husband's child? She told me they were having an affair. I was in shock for a week."

"Mrs. Fleming, are you telling us that you knew about Lisa Given's affair and pregnancy?"

Mrs. Fleming fingered the tea drawer.

"Yes, my husband explained he took a slight detour from our marriage and there was a possibility his genes were deposited elsewhere. He said there wasn't an affair. There was a brief fascination. I believed him. I told you he liked modern. Lisa was modern, young, and pretty. She's not the first fascination and she won't be my husband's last. Of course, I assumed that Lisa would want money from us, and I approached her with my offer."

"What was the offer?"

"The offer was that she must leave my company immediately with four hundred thousand dollars. She refused. She didn't want to quit her job and she wanted much more. I changed my offer and let her know she could stay with the company, but no more fascination or affair allowed. I offered her five hundred thousand dollars and one thousand shares of stock. She refused my second offer. A few weeks went by with no response. She was rude to me. I took matters into my own hands. I didn't want to bother my husband with a trivial matter. I sent her a note that I was done with her. She could take my offer or leave it. *I didn't care.*"

"Mrs. Fleming, what amount did she want?"

"Five million. I have the money, but five million for a baby is too much."

Candace agreed. "You have the money and five million is a lot of money. The amount borders on extortion. Or a motive for murder."

"We travel in high circles, dear. Five million isn't so much. Some of our advertisers pay us a good salary for news spots. I only mentioned my deal and didn't think about extortion. My offer was for services for the baby. Now that Lisa is gone, we won't have to pay for more services. See, there's no motive here. I tried to help Lisa."

Detective Moon couldn't understand rich people like Mrs. Fleming.

Mrs. Gene Fleming poured herself more tea.

"I want you to know our company has hired a psychic to find Ali. We decided to try to help with the investigation to show our viewers that we care. The psychic has seen a view of a raven in a pinyon pine tree."

Doug interrupted. "There's a lot of those types of trees in the southwestern United States, western North America, and elsewhere."

Mrs. Fleming smiled, "I know there are. The psychic mentioned another view. The raven held a piece of something in its mouth."

Doug intervened, "Dead mouse."

Mrs. Fleming laughed.

"Probably a large roof rat. A mouse is hardly worth chasing."

Candace wondered about the psychic. "We appreciate your providing us with this information. However, we must ask you a difficult question. Do you own a gun with a silencer?"

"Good heavens, where did that question come from. I have guns but a silencer would mean a felony conviction in California. My grandfather and father owned all sorts of guns. At one time, we put the older guns in frames on the wall in the library. Decoration changes and the guns went out of vogue. They were packed away. Besides, I didn't care if Lisa lived or died. I know that sounds cruel. I certainly wouldn't take the time or effort to chase or kill her."

Doug mentioned, "Lisa was mouse theory."

"Exactly. Your partner is wise."

"Did you feel this way about an Emily Lund, whether she lived or died? She was an employee of your father's that was murdered?"

Mrs. Fleming was visibly shaken. Her recovery was miraculous. She sipped her tea.

"Now, really, that was a long time ago and was very unfortunate. We don't control what happens outside the walls of our business. The ski resort was the company sued. Or the family attempted to sue them. I'm not sure if they were successful. Besides, the one murder has nothing to do with this current case. It seems to me that you two detectives are on the wrong course. I know your boss and the media are pushing for a closure. It doesn't mean that you can barge into my home and make accusations."

"We're not yet making accusations. We're trying to find a killer. You told us Lisa was pregnant. Did she mention anyone else who knew of her dilemma?"

"No, I didn't ask. I didn't care."

Candace was about to get up and leave.

"You don't think my husband killed her? No, he wouldn't be so foolish. There are no golf clubs in prison."

"We're talking to everyone we can. Right now, we are reviewing all the evidence."

"Good. Make sure you have all your marbles together. I'll inform my husband about your visit. He can contact the lawyer. Our company lawyer is our private lawyer and is paid handsomely."

"Yes, maam. Thank you for your time and the tea lunch. I'll put my card on your tea cart. You can call me if there's anything else."

Doug was glad to stretch his legs. He remembered a fast food drive-in down the road. He was hungry and needed a bathroom break. Candace felt the same way.

"Good day."

Mrs. Fleming was still as a mouse after they left. She pushed the tea cart back to the corner.

Then Mrs. Fleming called her psychic. The raven held the key. There must be more information. She would ask Ben again about the bird handler's current address and phone. Ben would know the company and owner. She called Ben's phone and he was out for the day. Mrs. Fleming didn't leave a message. She found Hector's number. Her bridge women arrived per her maid. The tea cart was cleared.

Mrs. Fleming wouldn't tell the detectives any thing more from the psychic. They weren't believers.

## 24 Second Interview with Ben

**Detective Constantine decided** to take the lead for the interview with Ben Blake.

"Hello, Ben, we've come back to talk with you. We found that you were in Aspen at the time of Lisa Given's murder. Do you have an alibi?"

"Boy, you get to the point fast. I was invited to the poker game with Mr. Fleming. Something came up at the last minute and I had to bow out of the game. Mr. Fleming found an alternate and wasn't bothered in the least by my no-show. As for an alibi, I have a good one. I got lost and was driving around the area, trying to find my way back to the apartment of my friend. He lives in an area of dead ends and twisting roads unknown to GPS. You can see the mileage on the car receipt."

"Did you see Lisa Givens or Ali Zarin while you were in Aspen?"

"No, I see enough of those two bossy females at work. Why would I want to see them on my own time?"

"We understand you are not friends with Ali. We didn't know you disliked Lisa."

"Well, they were both bitches to me. I've been with the company the longest and one of them gets promoted. I figured Lisa was next."

"Bitches enough to want to harm them?"

"Are you arresting me or what? I can hate co-workers if I want. It doesn't mean I would kill them."

"No? We would like to see your collection of guns."

"You got a search warrant? I have rights."

Candace knew their request for one was denied. The judge didn't feel there was enough cause.

Candace replied, "We can go get one. I would think that you would deal with us rather than a group of unknown police with plastic gloves pilfering through your drawers. Unless you want them to see your private play toys."

The detectives could see the steam rise from the man sitting in front of them.

Doug stood up.

"Let's go. He's not going to cooperate with us."

Ben jolted out of the chair as if an electric shock prodded him.

"All right, I'll show you the collection. I hope none of my guns match the ballistics on Lisa. I told Gene he should never have hired those two women."

Candace took her time reviewing the guns and ammunition. There was no silencer, but she saw a magazine with one on the cover.

Ben saw her look. He put the magazine in a drawer.

"Did you ever shoot a gun with a silencer before?" said Doug.

"Yeah, sure. All real men try the gun. We want to make sure there's truth to the hype."

Doug handed him his business card. "Stick around. We may have more questions in your future."

The two detectives left.

"I don't think Ben is our mastermind in this murder. There's someone else with a much cooler persona. I haven't a grip on any names within the company. Did we miss anyone real obvious?"

Doug was driving the car and weaving through traffic. He didn't like to talk when the roads were busy. Candace let him focus on getting them far away from the area and back to safer grounds.

Candace thought about the missing weapon and knife. The killer's identity and gun were nowhere to be found.

Then she remembered they forgot to ask who the friend was in Aspen that Ben knew. Ben, Mr. Fleming, and some other person were around for the murder of Emily Lund and Lisa Givens. Any one of the three were viable suspects. Latin was in jail for Rad's murder. Candace kept reviewing the conversations in her brilliant mind looking for a discrepancy.

"Make that four suspects."

Doug turned on the radio to easy listening music.

"I agree with you. We need to find Ali to see if she will help set a trap."

"There's one person missing. Once I figure out the name, then we can approach her," said Candace.

"Do you think they'll let us use the space satellite to view the cabin?"

"No, we'd need more law than us involved in the case."

"What amount of security cameras do you think Grant has at his cabin? I bet there's lots of security."

Candace liked cameras. They didn't lie. "Do cowboys carry pistols and heavy gauge rifles?"

Doug laughed. "You'd look good with a gun holster and boots."

"Yes, to the massive security. He probably has more than one generator, too. And let's not forget his friends with more ammo. Ali's safe at the cabin."

Doug looked at the darkened sky. There's a weather front moving in. We better get to high ground.

"I like the rain. It helps me think like the egg salad."

Doug couldn't help himself. He opened the glove compartment. Inside, he tried to grab a small box of cinnamon donuts. Candace intercepted and opened the box. She ate one.

## 25 High Ground

Matlock drove his travel trailer on the road that Grant marked. The sheriff brought him the faxed map. He noted the garage and side building. This was the correct place. He looked down the gulley where water was flowing.

"I need to keep the trailer to the left. No, kidding. They could put in girders on that stretch of the road. This isn't the worst road I've been on."

Matlock patted his dog's head.

"Let's snoop around the place." The dog seemed to understand and stayed close to his owner.

Matlock was pleased with the garage. He could unhook the trailer and park the truck inside. The garage door opener worked. He used the punch lock to open the door to the building. Inside was a refrigerator filled with food. The freezer was full and the liquor cabinet.

He noted the couch folded into a bed and there were sheets, pillow, and blankets in the closet. The best part was the black leather recliner. There was a heavy woven rust-colored rug on the floor for warmth. He tried the chair out and knew this was where he was going to sleep. Matlock threw the dog bed on the couch. His dog looked at him.

"I know. The dog bones and your toys are in the truck. We'll go get them and bring in some guns from the trailer."

The dog bowl of water was filled, and the dog food emptied into a huge plastic bowl. After the dog was satisfied, he took his toys and laid down on his bed.

"I wish I could sleep but I have to get the trailer skirting on to keep the rain or snow out. You never know about the weather at this elevation."

He saw a larger version of his map on the wall. He studied the distance to the house and the emergency phone. He noted the satellite dish in the yard and the television.

Matlock finished his chores.

"Tomorrow, we'll go introduce ourselves to the missus. She knows we are here. Grant texted me. I think this will be a nice place for two to three months. Grant is paying me good money. I guess we're what you would call extra security."

The dog yawned.

"I'm going to fix me a drink and call my friend, the sheriff. Andrew said he wanted to be in on any fireworks. Grant told me to hold off for now on the invitation. I'm to only let him know that I'm on a job clearing some trees for the Evans boys. After the call, we're having T-bone steak. There's butter in the refrigerator and I saw a can of peas and mushrooms. Real potatoes, too. We like the red ones best."

The dog and Matlock settled in for the duration of the job. It was nice to have a real house. There was a small brick barbeque outside. He didn't need to get his rusty one out. There even was some firewood. He noted all the pinyons were cleared far away from the little homestead. He liked the idea of seeing someone coming from the windows. The gully and creek worried him. Grant told him no traps because Ali might step on them accidentally.

The morning arrived and he drove to the store using the map to pick up a tin of cough drops. He preferred the licorice ones and settled for lemon. His throat was always dry.

Next, Matlock drove to the cabin. He was amazed at how large the structure was on the outside. He heard the horses and went over to the barn.

Ali jumped with a fright, "Good grief. You are quiet. I didn't hear your truck or you. "Here puppy, come see the horses."

The dog respectfully stayed back from the barn stall.

"Good morning, Ali. Your husband told me they left two horses. I like to ride. We can check the fences together some day. I'll let you decide."

"Thank you. Would you like breakfast? I made a quiche and fresh bread. There's hot coffee, too. We use single cups."

"I saw that new-fangled machine on the counter in the house down the hill. Maybe you can show me how to work it. All the buttons did was blink."

Ali laughed. She met Matlock a long time ago at a barbeque. There was no reason to be on ceremony. They both were relaxed.

They ate breakfast and she showed him how to make coffee. They took their cups into the living room.

"I hear some trespasser used a knife and you were hurt. I'm sorry I wasn't there to flip it back towards him."

"It's hard to talk about the episode. There's more that I don't remember than what I do."

"They call what happens to a person in a tricky situation, brain freeze."

"Yes, I believe there was more than the brain that froze. I hope if I run into the killer again, I run."

Matlock drank his brew and petted the dog.

"We hope you don't run into him. However, your husband and I would welcome the challenge."

"Now that Grant and Milan are gone, I get scared."

Matlock knew Ali needed to ask him a question.

"I said scared. I really get way more than that. I guess the word is frightened out of my wits. Have you ever been that afraid?"

"Sure, I get a little scared walking into the laundry mart and forgot my soap."

He saw her laugh.

"I know the type of fear you're talking about. When I was in the military, they taught us our fear could help or kill us. So, when I get scared, I know what to do now."

"What do you do?" asked Ali.

"I tell myself the man isn't the bogyman. He's flesh and bones. A bullet will go through him the same as a bullet will go through me. I make a choice. I choose to live. He gets to die."

"You decide to be brave."

"There's no other way. When the time comes, you remember to be brave. Be brave for yourself and your wonderful husband."

"Thanks, Matlock."

"Now, show me your fancy computers with the camera screens. Then I'll go hunt for them outside. I'm supposed to figure out a way to make them less visible. Grant said there was wood in the garage next to the helicopter."

Ali showed him the computer screens and he disappeared with the dog while she loaded the dishwasher.

After a couple hours he returned to the house.

"I'll go in town tomorrow and get the paint colors your husband told me to buy. Then I'll paint my wooden blinds."

"Did you see the helicopter?"

"I surely did. That's one nice machine. I'll have you work the slide out tomorrow. It's too bad my flying license expired. I'll wait for Grant to give me a ride."

"There's guns hidden in the helicopter area. Remind me to show you them."

"Here we are talking calmly about trespassers and guns. If people heard us, they'd think we were the insane ones."

Ali laughed and gave him a hug.

"I'm glad we are two crazy friends."

"Shoot, I need to be getting along. See you tomorrow, Ali."

After he left, she called Grant. Her husband was happy there was someone nearby. His job was filled with busy court days. Grant would make some time in the future to see Ali. He knew he had been away from her for too long. He thought about having her fly to New York but decided against it. The reporters would be all over his condominium. The killer would eventually know where she was living. New York provided too many places to hide. When they cornered the killer, Grant wanted to be in open country.

Grant told Matlock about the Albuquerque Newspaper article. Matlock told him there was no need for explanation. He and the sheriff read the article at the ranch. They figured out quickly the woman named Alessandria was not a welcome guest at any of the Evans properties.

Grant told Matlock that he guessed correctly.

## 26 Mr. Johnson's Land

**Milan drove his** truck into town to pick up some items Grant requested. Then he drove to Mr. Johnson's place to deliver the final contracts to the man. He waited for Mr. Johnson to sign the documents and he gave a second original back to the man.

"I'm glad you let Grant buy the five-hundred acres. Grant wanted to be here but got caught in New York with continuance on a case."

Mr. Johnson looked at the box of groceries Milan deposited on his table.

"I appreciate Grant allowing me to stay here three to five years more. The oil company didn't want nothing to do with my living in the building. The oil company lost the opportunity to purchase my land. They can't have my land today or in the future. Good luck trying to find a piece as nice as this one. Grant will take good care of the place. We worked a good business sale on the deal. I'm satisfied. Thank you for the groceries."

"Anytime you need something, give the ranch phone a call. I saw your son, George. He's out of the living facility?"

"The facility called me and told me the boy was ready to come back home. They took a long time to educate him and get his medicine right. I put him in the bunk house. I don't know if I can handle him. He's very retarded sometimes and won't talk. I told the facility I would try for two weeks. If George can be trusted to stay here and help with chores, we'll be fine.

Otherwise, he will need to return to the facility. He keeps asking about Brownie."

Milan remembered George almost drowned trying to save his dog.

"I'm sorry to hear George keeps asking about his dog. I understand you lost him. Maybe you should find George a replacement."

"No, I don't have time to feed a dog."

"I understand. I need to check on the cabin. We'll see you around the first of the month."

Milan decided to drive the backroads to the cabin and see Ali. He was glad he purchased the cover for his truck bed. The wind resistance was better driving. Milan stayed overnight and returned to the ranch the next day. He talked with Matlock before he left. The cabin was quiet, and no trespassers were around.

Ali was glad to see Milan and watched him leave. There were a bowl of apples and oranges in the kitchen. Several were missing. She figured Milan took them. In the evening, she made chili for herself and drove down to give a covered dish to Matlock.

"Hello, Ali, you must be bored if you made me some chili. I will appreciate your dish."

"I put some roasted jalapenos in a plastic bag for you. They were drizzled in honey. I know you like your chili spicy sweet and may want to add them to the dish."

Matlock smelled the chilis. "I believe I'll eat them first. The chili will cool my throat down afterwards."

Ali smiled.

"I would have put some roasted apples in another dish except Milan took some of them and the oranges."

"That's funny, I saw some orange peels on the trail today. Milan wasn't anywhere near the trail. I wonder if we have an intruder."

"It's interesting that you said an intruder. I thought I saw something when I was painting downstairs. I looked at the computer screens and didn't see anything."

Matlock put the chili in the refrigerator.

"I'd like to stay tonight at the cabin. We need to figure out who's been on the property. There could be snoopy news people or somebody else. Either one is someone getting too close to you. We don't want anyone to recognize your pretty face. The sun is too low to ride horses and look at the property."

"Get your stuff. I can help ride with you tomorrow. Two people with guns are better."

"Amen."

Matlock hitched a ride with Ali back to the cabin. He would talk with Grant about building a small horse barn and fenced area so he could keep a horse handy where he stayed.

The next morning, they saddled the horses and rode to where the orange peels were thrown. He knew a killer wouldn't leave the peels. The fruit rind would have been buried and the area brushed to hide the ground. There was someone else on the property. Matlock looked at his garage and outer building. He turned the heat real low on the furnace.

"There should barely be any smoke coming out of the chimney. We need to go back. I'll go inside the cabin. You wait behind my trailer with the horses."

They turned the horses around and went back. Matlock took his gun and crept up to his door. He smelled chili and knew someone was inside. Slowly moving through the doorway, he saw a man eating his chili.

"Hands up and don't move."

The man dropped his spoon and lifted his hands.

"George Johnson, is that you, boy?"

The man's eyes lit up and he picked up his spoon and started eating. Matlock sat down.

"How did you get here, George? It's a mighty long ride by car. Weren't you in the boarding home? Or did you move in with your old man?"

"Truck. I rode in Milan's bed."

"I suppose my chili tastes good right now."

"My stomach was hungry."

"You probably ate some apples and oranges, too."

George shook his head.

Ali came to the door and stepped through into the room.

"Who is this person?"

"I'll call old man Johnson's place first. This is George, his son. He used to live in a facility. He must

189

have been at the Johnson property when Milan stopped there for the legal documents. Somehow he hitched a ride on Milan's truck and landed at the cabin."

Matlock went to the window to make the call.

"George, we need to return you to your dad."

"You have a dog."

"Yes, her name is Birdie."

"Birdie and Ali."

Ali looked at Matlock in alarm.

"She's on the news. Ali is missing."

Matlock knew there would be some explaining to old man Johnson. He went to the refrigerator and pulled out two colas.

"I'll drive George home and talk with his dad. You take the horses back. I'll let Grant know we have a potential leak. Let's hope George stays at his dad's place and not the living facility."

Ali bit her lip. She watched George play with Birdie.

"He needs a dog."

"I'll see what I can do on that score. I know old man Johnson doesn't like dogs. Maybe we can get a goldfish or cat."

George said, "I like cats."

"Well, I'll be darned. A cat shouldn't be too hard to find. There's a pet store on the way home. George, you want to see if they have any kitties?"

"Kitties are little cats."

Ali waved at the two men and she moved the horses toward the cabin following the fire break. She wondered if Mr. Johnson liked cats.

## 27 Alessandria at the Ranch

**The red SUV** drove into the ranch parking space. Milan recognized the vehicle as belonging to Alessandria. He was confused as to why she was at the ranch. Grant was in New York and failed to warn his brother about the designer. He waited until she knocked on the door.

"Hello, Milan, aren't you going to let a lady inside. I need to talk with Grant. My schedule has opened plus there is a wonderful estate sale with items he may be interested in purchasing."

Alessandria moved around the rooms as if she owned the place. She stopped in her tracks.

"Look at you, cowboy grunge personified."

Milan looked at his stockings. He left the caked mud boots in the mud room.

"Alessandria, I look like this ninety-five percent of my day because I drive cattle, feed the cattle, take care of horses, and the watering, not to mention fix fences. I'm sorry I can't be on the fashion runway today.

"Maybe I should have called so you could have dressed better. Aren't you going to offer me a glass of cold?"

Milan cut avocados and cucumbers, opened a can of coconut milk, and Greek yogurt. He deposited the ingredients in a new blender Grant ordered.

"Where did you get the avocados?"

"You know Grant, he ships from anywhere. Last month, it was bananas. The month before that, it was pecan nuts. I have no idea what he's ordered for next month, other than a note arrived in my email from some citrus company. Grant sent me a note to give the citrus to the Sheriff's wife. The woman cans fruit was the only response in his note. A case of canning jars arrived in the mail. I assumed they were part of the citrus package. The avocados arrived two days ago. I've been busy cooking hamburgers with avocado, dip and chips, and shakes. Here, you need to try the cold green blend. The recipe is spa-quality to soothe the soul."

She looked at the glass with distaste. She wanted to ignore Milan. Grant was strange in the food zone. She was a party to his strange conversations with chefs in the restaurants they ate. Alessandria was bored with the ingredients of recipes and odd shipments. She believed Milan's story. The sheriff's wife did can.

"Suit yourself."

"Oh, all right, pour me a glass. And no, I don't can. I do not want to see citrus, nuts, or anything arrive on my doorstep. Recipes are burned."

Milan handed her the concoction. "I wrote my recipe down if you want to put the ingredients in the newspaper."

Alessandria tasted the drink and drank half the glass. She sent him a very angry look.

"The green drink recipe is destroyed. No jars, I get it." Milan quickly put the blender container top in the dishwasher. He was used to women being angry. Somehow, he brought the worst out in women.

She needed to get back to her business reason for the visit.

"We need to repaint the walls and redesign some of these spaces. The rooms are looking out of date. New lighting would work. What about the bedrooms?"

Milan let her wander through the house. He heard her gasp at the caked mud and other assorted items on his cowboy boots near the laundry machines.

"Your mud room is disgusting. You should put in a drain to wash evil things away."

Milan was starting to enjoy himself. The woman in his house hated dirt. He tried hard to remove the dirt. The ranch contained massive quantities of the stuff. The dirt was a freak of nature, naturally occurring. He couldn't control the wind or earth. Milan was exempt from the earth's powers. He parked his frame in front of the visitor.

"That's the best designer advice I've ever heard from your pretty lips."

Alessandria didn't like his tone and she moved away from the dirty cowboy.

"You need a bath."

Milan knew when women wanted. Alessandria was there. "I'd take one except you're here. I walk around naked."

"Go ahead, I've seen worst."

Milan was exasperated by the woman. She was like the rest of them. His bravery deflated. He knew his brother wasn't into the woman. He was delirious about Ali.

"I was joking about getting naked. I wear a towel. I don't do cave stuff. Maybe you can buy me some French soaps that will make me smell good."

"Lavender. You have the weed in your yard. Just rub some real hard on your body. You can burn the stems with your boots."

"I'm not touching lavender. Alessandria, you do try people with your words. It's no wonder there aren't any friends in your life. I'm trying to make conversation and getting nowhere. Why don't you take a hike? I'll go buy myself some pretty soaps. There's plenty of stores with pretty women where I can ask. I don't need your advice. Are you done checking Grant's ranch? I see why he's decided to disappear when you come around. You might be looking for someone in his bed sheets?"

Alessandria frowned at Milan.

"I didn't check his sheets. The rooms smelled clean."

She was getting nowhere with the brother. He was being particularly antisocial. The man had testosterone working against him. She thought there was no wonder he didn't have a girlfriend. He pissed her off.

"No, I'm going to ignore your comments. I'm checking the design possibilities that Grant needs. You mentioned looking for someone. I hoped to find Ali on the premises. She and Grant were close once. It would make sense that she was here. I have a friend in the newspaper business who would love a crack at her story. I'm here to offer her a deal. She could use my help."

"You don't even know Ali. The designer goods and estate sale were a ruse to get into Grant's hacienda? Not to mention, your insulting me."

"Milan don't be silly. I've brought the brochure for the estate sale. See, here is the document. We still have some time. You can mail the brochure to him."

She dug deeper in her purse and pulled out the paint and fabric samples. "Gold walls are so out now."

"I thought we painted and put new drapes in five years ago. The faux gold leather walls and drapes are barely dusty."

Alessandria went to the window and shook the drapes. Dust scattered across the light.

"Maybe we can get them cleaned. I'll talk to the cleaning lady. She should know where to take the drapes."

"And the walls? They match your mudroom."

Milan sighed. His brother's choice in choosing women was incredibly stupid. He saw right through Alessandria and her tricks.

"He's in New York, you can email him the document and swatches yourself. His plans on decorating are not under my realm or authority."

"All right. I'll also talk to him about this ranch and upgrading things. There may be people here in the future with cameras. You never know when reporters will descend. Grant will want his ranch to be a showcase of grandeur."

195

"I don't know about the grandeur thing. Alessandria, tell me you've not talked to a reporter?"

"Maybe I did talk to a friend, so what?"

"Grant likes his privacy, in case you've forgotten. The sign by the cattle gate says no trespassing. Be careful you don't push Grant out of your life. Right now, he's not interested in decorating. He's been home recently checking on real estate. I'm surprised you didn't know he was here."

"I don't know why Grant didn't tell me that he was at the ranch. That's totally absurd about real estate. He owns a massive quantity of land. There's no reason for him to waste his money. Whose land is he wanting to buy?"

Milan was worried he talked too much. "Grant does what he wants. Expansion is what he does. There is no reason for him to tell me anything. I like being out of the business end. I'm only the ranch hand. The mood and particulars of how he manages his businesses are above my sphere of influence. He's the lawyer guy and smart one. Maybe you should give him a call."

Alessandria looked perturbed. "Every time I call him, his line is busy. He used to answer all the time. Then Ali disappeared. Grant is now too busy. He told me there are heavy cases he's working. I don't believe him."

Milan looked at his watch.

"Grant is always busy."

The cleaning lady would be arriving shortly. Milan would be glad to have his laundry done because he was running out of blue jeans and shirts. He ordered more underwear online.

Another knock was heard at the front door. Grant let the cleaning lady into the house. He excused himself from his visitor and went with the cleaning woman to his building. Alessandria followed.

The laundry was shown to the cleaning woman and Grant was relieved when Alessandria exited his quarters.

"I'll be going now. You were right. Ali isn't here. If you see her, let her know she has a friend. A friend of Grant's is a friend of mine."

Milan walked her to the SUV to make sure she left the ranch. He watched her pass the cow gate.

He said to himself, "What a bunch of bullshit? Be wary of women in red heels. They'll grind you to the ground or push you off a cliff."

Milan was so disgusted with the visit with Alessandria, he forgot to tell Grant until much later about the unscheduled home tour. He took his boots out the back porch and sprayed them clean.

The cleaning lady left and there were newly washed items folded on the dryer. Milan put them away in his chest of drawers. The place was dusted and clean. He looked in the refrigerator and groaned. Tonight, would be dinner at Rosie's.

## 28 Prison Slip

**There was a flu** epidemic at the prison where Latin Dooley was being held. He was moved to the medical ward. While there, he went into convulsions, and Mr. Dooley was transported to a local hospital with two prison guards. Mr. Dooley became conscious and was uncontrollable. The doctor couldn't find anything wrong with him. The doctor made the decision to send Mr. Dooley to a mental hospital. Within the hour, he walked off the facility and was currently missing.

Detective Moon read the report and threw the papers at her partner, Doug.

"Huh, are you kidding me? They put a murderer in a mental hospital. I bet his lawyer had something to do with the transfer."

"No shit, Sherlock."

"Hey, don't swear at me. You're acting mad."

"Yes, I'm very mad. We worked hard to ensnare Mr. Dooley. He walks out of the mental ward. See, I told you he was smart. He plays everyone."

"Should we go to the prison?"

"No, I might get arrested for my ugly thoughts."

"Wow, you are mad."

Doug picked up the paperwork and laid the note in his basket for the secretary to scan. He'd file the document later under Prison flubs_Dooley_Date.

"He must have found someone to pick him up. The only person I can think that knows him is one guy."

"The white van looks like any of the other food vans driving in and out of the prison. A cheap stick-on sign would make entrance easy. Hector Hansen would know where Latin kept the van keys."

Doug remembered the van. "Why would Hector risk arrest?"

"We don't know for sure if it was him. However, I'm betting there's money connected to this plot. What if Mrs. Fleming paid Lisa Givens five million dollars? We need to go back to accounting, Ben, or Mr. Fleming to see if there's a trail. I believe Rad was murdered because our killer thought he knew where Lisa parked the cash."

Doug said, "If we can't find the initial check, we need to ask Mrs. Fleming or get a warrant on her personal account. It's difficult to take five million out of a bank at one time."

"I'm not thinking bank. They have a safe in their home. Five million would be easy to keep in the house. We assume there was money exchanged. Where would Lisa keep the money or with whom would she entrust part of the booty. She wouldn't keep the cash in one spot, or would she? The bags, of course. Remember what Latin told us. Lisa brought lots of baggage to Aspen. She kept the money with her at the rental."

Detective Moon answered her phone and listened to the officer for ten minutes.

"We'll be right there. Is she going to file an insurance report?"

199

Doug waited patiently for Candace to hang up the phone.

"Mrs. Fleming called the police to report a robbery. She told the officer she hadn't checked her gun collection in quite some time. They also disturbed her garden room. The tea cart drawer was open. Mrs. Fleming lost the key for the drawer a long time ago. Guess what she's missing?" said Candace.

"The same caliber gun that killed our victim."

"And an old silencer that might have been in the tea cart?"

"The tea cart where we ate those tiny sandwiches? How odd? You kept looking at the drawer thinking about salt. No wonder Mrs. Fleming was nervous. She knew the contents of the tea drawer," said Doug.

"Yes. She told the officer the silencer was not registered to her. The item was registered to her father. So, she technically didn't lie to us. However, when her father passed away, the property and personal contents became hers."

Doug couldn't believe they were in a room with an old gun and silencer. "Mrs. Fleming was splitting hairs on a donkey or a mouse."

"I'd say you are probably correct. She acted strange when I looked too long at the tea cart. At least we can have an opportunity to check the house for a wall safe. I'll take the lower rooms. You take the upstairs."

"What's my excuse for going upstairs?" asked Doug.

Candace gave him her banana. "The lower bathroom gets plugged accidentally."

Doug was glad her sense of humor returned. They left the office to visit an overly dramatic woman. Mrs. Fleming should have been an actress was what Candace thought. The scene was award-winning stuff.

Both detectives were able to check the walls when the lower bathroom toilet overflowed on the marble floor and hallway Persian rug. Mrs. Fleming went to find Consuelo or any other hired help and locate bathroom towels. Candace found the wall safe in the den. The two detectives also searched any older bank accounts that were under Ms. Fleming and her father. There was money recently withdrawn. The amount was five thousand dollars.

"Birdman money."

### XXXXX

The next morning, the police would find Latin Dooley in his underwear dead at his home from a bullet. The back of the garage floor was dug out and a large metal chest was open. There was nothing inside. Black paint was poured over a small hole. There were only Mr. Dooley's prints on the paint can and opener. They assumed Mr. Dooley was the person in the garage who dug the chest out.

The coroner was called, and police cordoned off the scene for a few days. A local museum took the stuffed raccoons and didn't want the birds. An auction was held, and the house was placed up for sale. The horsehair sofa went to the dump with the newspapers.

There was no money in Mr. Dooley's bank accounts. The bank clerk told the detectives the man withdrew the proceeds the day before. Mr. Dooley was excited about a trip to Acapulco, Mexico. The detectives found the brochures in a suitcase in the closet with his ticket and passport. Mr. Dooley wasn't going to make his flight with stolen id and credit cards. The detectives noted the writing in black marker on the brochures.

No one came forward to claim the body and Mr. Dooley was buried in a section of the cemetery where there were no fancy headstones or urns for flowers. The neighbors complained about the stop sign. The county put in a new one. A llama farmer moved onto the property and quickly put up fences. The house was used to store feed.

## 29 Money Secured

**The two killers** congratulated themselves at retrieving the other part of the money.

"How did you know Latin stole the other half of the five million?"

"Mr. Dooley was the only one around the lodge that knew Lisa and Ali. He more than likely saw the two women leave their rental home. He was obsessed with Ali. Obviously, he found the carryall with the cash in the bedroom closet. Lisa paid us our share. Once I was able to free Latin from prison, I waited. He went to his garage and was taken aback when I arrived. The money was stacked next to the paint can. He wanted to share the money."

"I'm glad you took your time and had the tenacity to wait. The old man was a fool and a stalker. I saw him come out of the woods around the photo shoot. He was stalking Ali. I had to leave to get ready for the job. I could never figure out why you hung out with the old man. He was cheap and Latin's greed killed him. Maybe we would have let him live. We might have shared the money to keep him quiet."

The tall man contemplated his next move.

"Sometimes cheap people can be used. I liked to match my brilliance to his. He wasn't bright about money, only birds. He called me birdman once. Now he's dead birdman. We're free to leave with all the money. I doubt we would have shared."

"No, man, she saw me. We have one more job to do," whined the second person.

"Ali Zarin may not remember anything about her attacker. It's your fault. Why didn't you finish her with the gun? There was plenty of time to use the gun again and enough bullets. No, you used a knife. Wrong move."

"The knife was easier. We don't even know if she's alive and living in New Mexico. She could be anywhere."

"New Mexico is the only place she could be. I've looked at some of her other vacation spots. Mrs. Fleming told you about an article in an Albuquerque Newspaper. I read the article. The article was convincing. Ali may be staying with an old boyfriend now that Rad is out of the picture."

"Why work so hard when all we have to do is wait. Let the police find her. They might even arrest Ali for Lisa's murder."

The tall man was getting bored. He looked at his watch. Today was Tuesday. His calendar was displaying the time for his meeting.

The shorter man kept talking. "I'm lucky to have seen Latin Dooley enter Lisa's cabin and walk out with a bag. The bag was red with pink nametags. How dense can a person be taking a female's bag? That's when the lightbulb went off. My getting lost saved our butts. Otherwise, we wouldn't have known where the other half of the money went. Latin's thievery and Lisa's help were our reward. No, we must find Ali."

"Stop the whining about Ali. I hate when you do that to me."

The tall man looked at his partner. "Was Lisa surprised when you shot her. Tell me again what happened."

"I don't want to talk about the murder. I wish that I hadn't decided to be the courier for the transaction. It wasn't my fault the biker didn't arrive."

"No, this time things weren't your fault."

"Mrs. Fleming wanted to make sure her heavy package was delivered. She would get upset if I didn't get her package out the door. I got suspicious when the address was to a PO Box. I waited and saw Lisa Givens pick up the document. She sat in her car. I crept closer. She was so busy counting the green money, her eyes didn't see me. I couldn't believe the stacks that were placed on the car seat."

"Green twenty, fifty, and one-hundred-dollar bills are a pretty sight," said the tall man.

"I followed her to her apartment. While she was in the shower, I read the document. She put the note on her table. Lisa was pregnant by the boss. I barely escaped from her apartment. I wish I never saw the document."

"Yeah, you killed her cause she wouldn't go out with you. I still don't get the knife on the other woman."

"I saw the knife in Lisa's room at the lodge and the handkerchief. I took both. The knife was personal. I hated Ali Zarin. She kept asking me questions about my other jobs. She asked about Idaho. Then she asked if I knew Emily Lund?"

"I hope you didn't tell her anything."

"No. I ignored her. I told her the newsroom was filled with young women in Idaho. I told her some of them were bitches. Ali stopped fishing for information."

"You're one real social guy. Or should I say sourpuss? You need to keep your feelings for women under wrap or else people will get suspicious."

The short man didn't like to be reprimanded.

"I still want to leave. The money is telling me to have myself a good time." The tall man looked at the bag of money. He was the one who made the arrangements. Lisa paid them half the money. He was guaranteed all the money. That's why Lisa was eliminated. He looked at his watch again.

Both killers were silent.

One of them was thinking about the money. There might be another way to get more greenbacks.

Ben told the tall man about Mrs. Fleming owning a specific caliber gun and a silencer. His gun and silencer shouldn't be used again. The tall man wondered why he wasn't told about the gun. This new revelation was a complication. He worried where the other person was leading him. He wrote down in his calendar.

*I don't care.*

The tall man looked at the words. He wondered why those words bothered him. Maybe it was the way the person said the words. He knew appearances were deceiving. He thought that he was the leader. Now he wasn't so sure. Taking his pen out of his pocket, he wrote *MF*.

The mastermind re-thought about the older gun. There were too many decisions to make. He needed some time. He would rethink about Ali Zarin.

"I have to leave. We'll talk later."

The tall man was thinking about his partner. He didn't care. Ali didn't know his name. Still, there was the raven. The raven liked Ali.

"Would she come looking for the raven? Would she guess who he was and where the connection existed between the killers? Ali saw him in the elevator at the lodge."

The mastermind thought about what Rad told Ben in his final moments. There was more blackmail money to be earned. Lisa shared information with Rad, much more than they previously thought. The decision to kill Rad was the right move.

Nothing was agreed or decided.

Ali Zarin was given a reprieve.

## 30 Grant's Arrival

**Three months passed.** Matlock must move to his next job. Ali and Grant were stuck with having to decide about their next direction. They waved to Matlock as he drove out of their driveway.

"I'm glad he was here. He cleared quite a bit of trees for me. I gave him a bonus so he could have a good time at the casino."

"Yes, we enjoyed his company. I loved his old stories. He encouraged me to take some drawing lessons. He specifically mentioned the human face. He told me if I doodled a little, my brain would unfreeze."

"He's right. Your hand may consciously pick a face profile. Let's go in and discuss our next move."

Slowly, they entered the cabin. "If we call the police and let them know you are here, do you want to go into protective police custody or help with a plan to catch Lisa's killer and your attacker?"

"I'd like to end this madness of waiting. I know Latin is dead. The police believe he killed my boyfriend. Lately, I thought he might have been Lisa's killer and my attacker but I'm not so sure. There are things that don't jive. The man in the red outfit and mask was taller than Latin. Latin didn't know my boyfriend. Rad would have mentioned him."

"I'm not a detective and there's no use for you to try to unscramble two murders. Let's hope the killer is done."

"We'll call Detective Moon in the morning. I'm bushed from my flight and drive."

208

"You're too tired?"

"No, not that tired. We have some catching up to do in the love-compartment. Maybe I should wait a few weeks before contacting the detective."

"I'm into waiting. We need space and time to be man and wife."

"Let's agree."

"Do you think we can get a dog? I really liked having Matlock's dog here."

"I'll have Milan check around with the local dog breeders. He can send us pictures."

"Good, let's celebrate with some wine."

After they drank their glasses, they took a shower together. Both were toweling when the power went out. The house was in darkness. The generators started and the lights went back on.

Grant threw his pants and shirt on and grabbed his boots.

"I'll check the power. You call the electric company to make sure they are aware of the power failure. If not, then we have trouble."

The power came back on after twenty-five minutes. The power company repaired the disruption.

Both fell into bed relieved the emergency was over. Ali was glad she reacted appropriately and didn't freeze. She felt her scar and knew she was stronger. Grant was there and she tried to be brave.

Grant kept his promise about not being tired. The time together added strength to their union. They talked about their future together and building a family. Ali felt the cabin was her home.

Grant moved the buffalo fur and arrows to the helicopter office and bought a beautiful painting of purple hills. She liked to look at the picture in the morning while they drank coffee in bed. City life and her job were no longer a part of her world. Making a home was more important.

They floated in the hot tub, cooked fish purchased from town, and fried chili peppers for freezing.

One day a local woodcarver installed a sign. They talked about a name for the cabin. Ali waited until the carver left. The sign read, *Raven's Rest.* There was a carved pinyon tree with a raven. Underneath was lettering, *Evans Cabin.* There was space for Ali and Grant's name which they would add later.

Ali was pleased.

"The sign looks mystical."

"The size is absolutely correct. You wanted larger. The location next to the rock is good. We can have the landscaper move some of the plants, so they slope away from the sign."

"Your idea suits me fine. Does this guy make baby beds?'

Grant looked at Ali in surprise. She saw the look.

"Not yet, but some day."

Grant was relieved. He wasn't ready to be a father. Their lives were too rocky from the murders.

"I called the wood carver and he picked up strawberries for me. I hoped you would make me some jam."

"There's cream cheese in the refrigerator. You clean the berries and I'm going to try this new recipe for bread."

"Maybe we can take a break when the bread rises. The jam will cook quickly while the bread is in the oven."

"Maybe we can take a break."

"You are the only woman I want to hold and make my dreams come true."

"And you're the only husband I want to kiss, cook, and hide from prying eyes."

"Your kiss is what started this whole thing with us, that and the sweet strawberry jam."

"The new drapes in the master bedroom will turn out the lights."

Grant took his wife by the hands. There wasn't a minute to waste. He led her to their bedroom and privacy.

Ali knew her husband. He was making his move. She was letting him in. Both were up for the challenge. If the bread burned a little, there was a second loaf Ali left out.

"The drapes are working, except I can't see your smile."

"Trust me, Grant, when you hold me. I'm smiling."

# RAIMENT RED AND A RAVEN

Grant felt free when he was with Ali. He was glad she finally came home and there would be a forever.

## 31 Missing Employee

**Their employees always** took a month's vacation every year. The news station wasn't concerned until a week later.

Mrs. Fleming called Detective Moon's office and she picked up her phone on the first ring.

"Mrs. Fleming, what can I do for you?"

"Yes, I suppose you have call recognition on your end. We didn't want to pay for the service at our home or office."

"You didn't call me to complain about your telephone arrangements. I know the police are trying to locate your gun. They do have your security video. However, the person wore a mask which makes our job more difficult."

"I have another matter of importance. I wanted you rather than the local police. You appear much more capable of dealing with strange developments."

"What strange development?"

Mrs. Fleming hesitated, and Candace could hear someone in the background encouraging the woman to make the call. The detective assumed the person was Gene Fleming.

"It's about our employee, Ben Blake. He went on vacation for four weeks. The time of his absence is now five weeks. He always returns from vacation in a better mood. We appreciate the fact that he revives himself. You know, sometimes the man could be a real downer. His grumpiness affected everyone on his floor."

"I'm sorry to hear that Mr. Blake is missing. I'll transfer you to someone who can complete the missing person report."

"No, don't transfer me. I don't want to do a report like I'm responsible for him. We're just his employer."

"I see. Is there anything else that I can help you with today?"

"Yes, that's why I called. There was a delivery. The package was private."

Candace motioned Doug and she turned the speaker phone on.

"You see, Ben took the package delivery to the PO Box rather than the courier company. The courier company sent me a letter of apology that their biker was in an accident. It never occurred to me that Ben would deliver the package."

"What was in the package to make you so upset?"

"The five million dollars in cash."

"What five million? Oh, no, you didn't send Lisa Givens the money?"

"Yes, I caved in to her request. Lisa told me my husband might leave me. She said he wanted the baby to be adequately taken care of. I'm an old woman. I can't attract men anymore. Besides, I like my husband despite his faults."

Doug was listening on the speaker phone. He rolled his eyes.

"Mrs. Fleming, your husband knows about your payment?"

"I didn't say that he knows. My husband wouldn't understand. I'm handling my affairs. I think Ben might have opened the package and saw the money and note I left."

"You put a note in the package?"

"Yes, and I indicated the amount. I wanted Lisa to understand this was a one-time deal for the baby. I didn't give her the money. I don't give a crap about her. I've told you that information before."

"I do remember you telling me exactly your feelings about Lisa."

Candace worried what would happen when the police revealed who the father might be of Lisa's baby. She knew they were checking databases.

"I'm scared that Ben ran into Lisa's killer because of my package. That might be why he's missing. Ben knew about the money. Now the killer knows my name. I might be his next victim. Money can be a powerful motive."

"Yes, I understand your idea about money. I'll see if the police can provide someone to watch your home for a few days. We'll ask the police to check Ben's apartment and the hotel where he went on vacation. Do you possibly know where he went this year?"

Mrs. Fleming tried to remember the place. "He kept brochures taped on his desktop. That way, everyone could see he was having a grand time. This time the places were, I think, the Bahamas. Yes, most specifically the Bahamas. Can your police people stay longer than a few days?"

"I'll let your husband know you're nervous about Ben missing and we'll keep him UpToDate on any information we find about your employee."

"Thank you. Oh, there is one more item. I did tell Ben about Ali's boyfriend, the one in New Mexico. I was sure the two of them would make it together. I was so impressed by Grant Evans. I was reminded of their relationship when I read an article in the Albuquerque Newspaper. The nice designer woman, Alessandria Morgan, revealed Ali's name."

"Yes, we saw the article. Good day, Mrs. Fleming."

Candace hung up.

"I wonder who was in the room with Mrs. Fleming?"

Doug waited.

"We need to schedule a visit to New Mexico after you deal with missing persons."

"I should wait until after we check Ben's apartment."

"No, we'll let the police handle things here. I want to be on the plane tomorrow. The time has come to talk with Ali."

Doug rushed off to make the arrangements. Candace couldn't believe they were getting close to the mastermind killer. She knew she better be well-prepared.

Candace picked up her phone. The call should come first.

"Grant Evans here."

"This is Detective Moon. We have a new development in the case. We'd like to fly down and discuss our case. There is a killer who may know where Ali is located. I'd like to catch the SOB."

Grant hung up his phone and redialed Matlock.

Matlock stopped his rig at a parking pull over space. The rig was turned around and he headed back the opposite direction. When the rig was safe, Matlock called his friend to let him know there was an emergency. The friend was all right with the delay. Then Matlock contacted Sheriff Cray. His only message on the phone was, *showdown happening at Evans cabin.*

## 32 No Show

**The police, Grant,** Sheriff Cray, Matlock, Detectives Moon and Constantine, and Ali waited for a week after the announcement of her return to life. A video was done at the cabin and sent to Ali's boss. The news media event was televised in Los Angeles by her boss. The ratings hit the roof as she told her story.

The trap was set to catch the killer at the cabin. Trees and special gear were used as cover to hide. There were marksmen stationed around the perimeter. They didn't want the man to escape. The police plans were wasted. The killer was a no show. The police were certain the killer would appear.

The killer did appear. Only thing wrong was the location. The body of Ben Blake was eventually found in his bathtub, drowned, in a Los Angeles apartment. Some sleeping pills were found in the medicine cabinet. The police weren't sure whether the death was accidental. There was a revolver, bullets, and silencer found in Ben's hands. The police were checking the ballistics and the weapon match.

The detectives and police disbursed from the cabin grounds. The detectives flew back to LA to investigate Ben's apartment.

Grant stayed another week to calm Ali down.

She didn't like Ben but wondered who got close to him. Ali only remembered some of Ben's past conversations. She wasn't much help to the police. She did say he was the correct height of her attacker. The police went through Ben's apartment and found no further evidence. There was a box full of brochures from his past vacations. The brochures were marked in black marker with the dates. The box was put in the police evidence room.

Eventually, Grant returned to New York City. Sheriff Cray left to drive back to his job. Matlock was scheduled to leave in the morning.

Ali was glad Lisa's killer was found and her attacker. She looked at Ben's image and printed the photo. With her pencils, she put him in a red parka and goggles. Then she did a closeup without goggles. His eyes were the same as her attacker. She was satisfied there was closure to her recent terror. Ali threw the images in the garbage. She didn't want to be reminded of her nightmare.

Matlock stayed the night on the cabin grounds and started talking to his dog.

"There's a story about a shepherd crying wolf, wolf so he would get people to come and guard his flock. Each time the people came, there was no wolf. Eventually, the people stopped coming. The wolf was super smart. The wolf waited and waited. Are you with me in the story, dog?"

His dog barked.

"Sure, you are. We've seen a wolf track on the property. The wolf hides from our view. We know the wolf is there. We wait. Why do we take our time?"

The dog whined and put his paws over his ears.

"I know you know the ending. There's always a big bang when we catch the wolf. We take our time because we're smarter. The wolf comes back after everyone is gone."

The dog's ears twitched.

"I'm thinking we have a trespasser who thinks like a wolf. The thing is there is no reason for me to stay. Yet, my gut tells me otherwise. Sheriff Cray was feeling the same way. He told me he was staying tonight at a local inn and driving back tomorrow. Sheriff Cray didn't want to scare Ali, so he didn't tell anyone except me. His gut was talking to him."

The dog yawned.

"A flat tire would be a good thing. I looked at the air in the trailer tires. Maybe we could just say they looked low. Then we could stay another day. What's one more day, huh, Birdie?"

His dog wagged his tail. Matlock knew he made the right decision. The wolf was approaching Matlock's turf. He would be ready. He already laid the traps on the creek side. Matlock probably should have set up bombs on the road. Bombs would have been more successful. He regretted leaving the dynamite at the Evans ranch. He could see the wooden box in the garage. Matlock should probably let Milan know about the box.

Matlock went into the garage. He pulled some boards off the wall and took out his special rifle. Then he placed the scope on the clip. Going back inside, the box of shells was placed on the kitchen table. Shells were loaded into slots on a leather strap. The strap was made to hold half a box. He fit the strap around his chest and was pleased how comfortable the bullets felt. He remembered the last time he wore the belt. He was hunting elk in Montana. The sight on the gun was a piece of perfection. Matlock hit the target every time. The holes were an inch apart on the target board. Matlock counted them, "Twelve, three, six, and nine o'clock."

Ali, too, was feeling edgy. There was something out in the pines. She could feel evil. There was no way to contact her husband. He was on an airplane. She was glad he was out of harm's way.

This was her fight. Ali slept in her clothes. Her boots and jacket were next to the bed. The gun holster was not empty. Several more bullets were put in her pockets. She zippered the pockets shut. She wanted to be brave and ready.

XXXXX

A tall man earlier in the week was in the hardware store in a city close to Johnson's ranch. A person named George was waiting for his dad while he watched the television. There was a bag of cat food in his hands and the man was eating popcorn. The tall man sat down next to George on the wrought iron bench. He quickly assessed the man's lack of intelligence.

"Boy-man."

The tall man almost moved away.

There was a picture of Ali Zarin on the news. George became excited.

"Ali, Ali."

The tall man said, "You know Ali. She's your friend. She's my friend, too. I have a present for her but don't know where she lives."

"I know. She made chili."

"I like chili. Maybe she can make me some."

"Don't eat the peppers. Too hot."

The tall man looked, and George's dad was busy at the key counter. The hardware boys kept paging through the key book.

"Your dad must have a very old key. They are hard to find to make a new one. Ali is hard to find. Where did you say you saw her?"

"Evans cabin."

"I don't recall where the Evans property would be. Ali is at the cabin. You're an amazing person to have figured this out. Your dad must be proud of you. What is your name?"

"George Johnson."

"Is the Evans cabin far from here?"

"My dad likes me. He helps me buy my kitty food. She stays in the bunk house."

"How far, George?"

"My dad told me ninety miles or more."

The tall man took out his map. He opened the map and drew a circle with his red pencil. The center point was the city they were in."

The boy-man knew how to look at maps. George pointed a spot. The tall man drew an *X*.

"Thank you, George. Take good care of your kitty. There are wild animals in the trees. Here's a dollar for the pop machine."

George ambled off with his cat food and selected the cola. When he turned around, the tall man was gone. He was disappointed. The tall man didn't give his name. George couldn't tell anyone about the encounter with the man without a name. He quickly forgot the stranger. His dad came with a key in a bag and he paid for their items. George went home to his kitty. He made sure the doors were locked with the new key. George didn't want wild animals to get in his bunk house. The tall man was scary. George hugged his kitty in the night.

The tall man made a phone call.

"I've found Ali Zarin."

He talked for five minutes and hung up.

A few days went by and George ran into his dad's kitchen. Outside was still dark.

"Phone, Matlock."

Mr. Johnson found his cell phone in the bedroom.

"What is it now, boy? You're up mighty early."

His dad dialed and talked with Matlock a few minutes. He handed the phone to his son.

"Scary man at hardware place."

"Whoa, slow down, George. There are people who look scary sometimes." Matlock was hurrying to put his shirt and pants on. The dog was dancing around him.

"Ali. The tall man asked about Ali."

Matlock sat up.

"You have my full attention, George."

"A map. He drew a map of Evans cabin."

"No."

"Ali. Where's Ali?"

"George, you rest easy. I'll go find her and keep her safe. You did good in calling me. Thank you."

George sat back with his kitty. His dad patted his hand. George wasn't stupid. He knew right and wrong.

"Bad man."

Mr. Johnson nodded. He hoped Ali would be okay. The warning was now in Matlock's hands.

"Why don't we buy Ms. Kitty a special bed next time we go to the hardware store. We can get some kitty litter and a pan for the main house. She belongs with the both of us during the day. In the meantime, there's an oil pan we can use and some wood shavings or better yet a bag of sand. There's also an old sheepskin rug in the closet. Ms. Kitty might want to check it out this morning. You might want to put a soft towel on top. Oh, bring some food. We got those plastic dishes in the cupboard for the water and eats."

George was happy. His kitty was purring. He handed Ms. Kitty to his dad and went to search for the items.

## 33 Ali Runs

**Matlock and Sheriff** Cray arrived in the sheriff's vehicle in the circular driveway of the cabin. The early morning light hadn't yet arrived. Matlock hoped the warning was received soon enough. Matlock noticed the doorbell blue light was out.

"The power is gone. This situation doesn't look good.

Sheriff Cray rolled down his window.

"No generator noise outside. We better check the house."

The two men carefully pulled their guns and crept slowly, checking the top floor and then the lower floor. They saw the sliding back door was open.

Matlock grabbed his phone. "No cell tower reception. She's running to the emergency phone. The phone is closer to where your camper is parked. We'll drive back and come from the bottom. We should run into Ali. She knows you're here and will move toward the other structure. Too bad the helicopter slide won't work without generators."

Sheriff Cray was putting more centerfire bullets in his pockets.

"Grant has a separate generator for the slide. It's behind the helicopter and runs on a private switch and line."

"That's good news. Should we take the machine up?" said Matlock.

"We don't know his gun power. The rotor engine and blades might be hit. I hate flying a broken machine. Scares the crap out of me every time."

Matlock nodded. "We're better on the ground. He's on the ground. The field levels out. Speed isn't important once we have him in our sights. I prefer absolute quiet."

The sheriff spoke, "I wonder if the power outage spooked Ali or she saw something on the computers before they crashed."

They arrived back at the lower garage and side building. The sheriff walked around the trailer and checked the door. The trailer door was still locked.

Matlock grabbed his rifle with scope. The sheriff reappeared and gave a thumbs up motion.

"You take the left flank and try to meet Ali. I'll stay here to make sure he doesn't get inside the garage. I'll be down hiding near the Creekside ridge."

"Just don't shoot me," said the sheriff.

"Naw, I know the color of that old rawhide jacket anywhere. The hat's even more tattered and stained. Then there's the tan boots."

The two men moved into their positions. Sheriff Cray saw Ali scrambling as fast as she could through the rock and pines. She slipped and fell. The sheriff stepped out from behind a tree to help her. A shot rang out. The bullet clipped the top of his hat.

"Damn, that was close. My favorite hat, too."

"I'll buy you a new one if we get out of this alive."

Ali scrunched down and was low under some bushes.

226

The sheriff waved her to keep coming. He moved his rifle and took a shot at movement on the hill. He hoped the bullet found a home in a warm body.

"The killer is here," gasped Ali. "We need to hide."

"George called Matlock. I'll explain later. You're on for the hat. I'm not dying today. Matlock is waiting. Let's get down the hill."

The two came around a large tree and stopped in their tracks. A man was standing in their way. He was dressed in camouflage. Ali didn't know the man.

"You both can stop."

Sheriff Cray saw the handkerchief tied around the man's leg. He did wound him. The sheriff knew the loss of blood would weaken the man. He also wondered where Matlock was on the hill.

"What do you want? This is private property and you're trespassing."

"You don't have to shout. I can hear you just fine old man."

The killer motioned to Ali and threw her a nylon rope.

"Tie his hands and throw his gun in the trees. Your gun, smart lady, goes in the weeds."

Ali complied.

"Now move, we're going to the building I saw from the phone. Were you surprised to hear no dial tone?"

The sheriff knew Matlock was their only source of help.

Upon reaching the bottom, the sheriff thought they would stop. Instead the killer motioned for them to move toward the creek. The sheriff knew the killer stole the horses out of the barn and was going to ride to his escape vehicle.

Matlock saw the three make their way down the gulley. He kept his distance when he saw the blood on the rocks. His only worry was that the killer would stop or arrive at his destination for escape. He kept trying to figure out where he could take a shot. He knew the terrain because he walked the area when he was there earlier. Matlock started moving to higher ground and was ahead of them. He heard the horses' nicker. He didn't have much time.

Ali stumbled again. Her feet were sore. She watched for any means of escape but knew she would not leave the sheriff. The sheriff bent down to help Ali.

The killer turned. Matlock took his shot. The killer's eyes were startled. Then they saw him tumble backwards down the hill to where the horses waited.

Matlock came down to Ali and Sheriff Cray.

"Can you make it back up the hill? I've got to track him to make sure he's dead."

Sheriff Cray said, "We'll make it. You catch him fast."

They heard the horse's hooves take off running.

"Shit, now I've got to call a horse. Go, now."

Matlock did his special whistle and the roan horse turned back to him. Matlock was happy the fool killer took his favorite horse.

"Hi, boy, good job. I don't have a carrot, but we'll get one later. We've got to catch a trespasser."

Matlock checked the ground. Horse and rider moved over the gulley toward a small lake. Matlock was aware of his area and every little sound. He stopped when he heard a twig snap. He lowered himself off his horse and tied the roan to a tree branch.

Ali and the sheriff should have arrived at the garage and outbuilding. The sheriff would try to reconnect the satellite dish wires. There were extra cables in the garage.

Matlock was used to hunting the enemy. An Indian friend taught him to look for the signs. A disturbed rock or branch or heel mark. He watched for any bird movement. He smelled the wind. There was rain coming soon.

Suddenly, Matlock saw a sleeve. Now was when he needed to decide. He knew the killer would shoot him without a second's warning.

"It's either you or me coming back up the hill. I choose me."

Matlock stepped out and fired at the arm. A bullet came at him from a different direction and grazed his left shoulder."

"Damn, I can't believe I fell for the oldest trick in the book. Only now I've got your direction. Trespassers are a dead giveaway. They never learned because they don't study their surroundings like us pros."

Matlock fired into the bushes. He waited and listened for movement. There was none. Matlock knew to wait. He slowly moved from his location. There was a clearing up ahead. The killer needed to cross in his line of sight. He dropped to the ground and crawled like a snake. He could slither over broken glass without making a sound.

The air smelled clean, and he checked the wind's direction. The other man wouldn't know he was there. Not even the wolves knew he was there. Matlock readied himself, taking time to position for the final show. He'd been ready his whole life for a good, suspenseful day. Too many of them were dull.

Suddenly, the killer moved. He started running with a limp down the hill. Matlock fired again. The bullet should have brought the man down.

"Bullet proof vest."

Matlock aimed for the feet and changed the shot. The head became the spot in the scope. Matlock hesitated as the man turned around. Fear was a good thing to see in a killer's eyes. There was no reason to wait. Matlock hesitated.

The man disappeared in a dip in the earth at approximately 450 yards. Matlock didn't move. He knew the man would reappear soon. The distance was further than he liked. The trespasser was approaching distance past Matlock's comfort zone and gun's range. A normal man would have given up.

"Wait for it."

He repositioned himself and raised the gun a fraction higher on the rock. The man would be running out of the dip. The man would be slower because of the rise in ground. A shape appeared. The man seemed invisible with the earth. The glare from the sun was blinding. A cloud moved in front of the sun.

# LINDA MCKOWN

There was no more time left for waiting. The man's shape blurred and solidified in the scope. Matlock knew there were only seconds left before the man would disappear into the trees. He couldn't let the man escape to trick and kill some other person. He thought about his friends. He remembered the talk with Ali and the fear today on her face. A woman shouldn't be that afraid.

Matlock looked again at the target. The rings on the target were clear. He knew how to change his world and kill a bad wolf. The trespasser touched something. Matlock took the shot. The bullet released from his gun at about 1200 feet per second. Matlock knew to wait for the delayed hit to strike at the target about 500 yards away. He counted a little past four seconds. He looked at the image. The image didn't fall. Matlock looked in his scope. The killer finally fell face forward. His right hand held and broke loose a pinyon branch.

"That was too close to the tree line. I'm getting too old to do this type of shot."

Matlock would have to explain his hand slipped. The feet were the real target. There was only one person who wouldn't believe him.

The wolves heard the boom and started to look for a hole to hide in. The sheriff also heard the one shot. He was glad he was not the person facing his friend. Matlock sometimes scared the crap out of the sheriff. His skills were hard to beat. Being in a shooting range was nothing like being in high country fighting the elements.

Matlock sat up and watched the fallen body. He didn't need to wait. He wanted to send a prayer up for his life. There was a reason to say grace. He whistled for his horse. The roan came up to him.

"See, I told you we'd catch him. Now we can get carrots. Not me. Those aren't my favorite things unless you hide them in stew. You stay still while I find the pinto."

Matlock could hear the police sirens in the distance. The place would be covered with them and reporters for days. He hoped Grant was on an airplane by now. Matlock didn't want to deal with the throng. He threw the dead body on the pinto, tied the man tight to the saddle, and walked back up the gulley.

Sheriff Cray was standing at the top of the ridge.

"Aren't you a good-looking sight? You look like a lost miner with his pack of gold. I see the trespasser caught you in the arm."

Matlock handed the roan's reins to the sheriff. They walked back to the house and tied the pinto horse to the railing by the garage.

"Ali, is she okay?"

"Yes, she's on the phone talking to Grant."

"Good. I've got to get some carrots for the roan."

Matlock went inside, cleaned his wound, and put gauze over the crease. He petted his dog and brought him out to feed the horses carrots. The dog respectfully kept its distance.

Police cars surrounded the place and almost moved to let the emergency vehicle through. There was no need for the vehicle. The killer was beyond help. The police did identify the body as Hector Hansen.

Detective Moon found out the dates of Ben Blake's vacation trips and matched the same dates Hector took the raven to his friends at the Wilderness Farm. The two killers knew each other, went on vacation together, and were friends a long time until money became a priority.

The writing on Ben's brochures matched the Acapulco brochure found at Latin's house. Ben somehow made the travel arrangements for Mr. Dooley using the same company.

The detectives were glad Matlock brought the mastermind and his schemes to a halt. They believed him about the feet being the target in his scope. Matlock was older and therefore, not responsible.

## 34 Case Wrap

**Detectives Moon and** Constantine arrived to meet with Ali. There were holes in their investigation.

"You knew about the murder of Emily Lund and talked with Ben Blake regarding the matter. Did he tell you anything?"

"Yes and no. He told me Mrs. Fleming owned a gun the same caliber and an old silencer."

"Why do you think he shared the information with you?" asked Candace.

"I believe he wanted to feel superior. He had information that I couldn't recover. It was his way of one-upping and snubbing me."

"Did you tell anyone this information?"

"Yes, I told Lisa about Blake's revelation."

Detective Moon showed her pictures of the gun and the bag of five million dollars found in the killer's motel room.

"We believe that Lisa Givens was killed because she blackmailed Mrs. Fleming about the gun and received money."

Ali didn't know why the killer came back to find her.

Detective Moon explained.

"Ben probably divulged the information he shared with you to Hector. You knew about the missing weapon. We think there's a possibility Hector planned to continue blackmailing Mrs. Fleming. You've also seen Hector before at the company with Ben and in

Aspen near the elevator or at the restaurant. He was the man Lisa was talking to when Latin overheard the conversation. Hector was Lisa's partner. She paid him half of the five million dollars. Lisa believed you would be the target. Hector and Ben turned the tables on her. Ben used the knife on Ali because she was one of those women that he called bitches. Ali didn't die. Hector knew he would be walking into a police trap in New Mexico. He waited in LA and killed his partner, Ben. Hector felt the entire haul of money was his. He was eliminating his pack from stupid people. Lisa, Latin, and Ben weren't up to his standards of intelligence."

Detective Moon let those facts sink in for Ali. Candace continued with her dialog.

"Ali was a loose thread that needed to be eliminated before Hector could take a travel vacation. Mrs. Fleming needed to be threatened so she would continue to pay him money. Stealing her gun ensured she would pay."

Doug took over while Candace drank her coffee.

"There were remnants of fabric and blood stuck inside the barrel of Mrs. Fleming's gun. No one cleaned the gun after it was used in a murder. This is the gun that killed Emily Lund in Idaho. We have arrested Mrs. Fleming for Emily's murder. We found Hector's blackmail note in Mrs. Fleming's bedside table. Mrs. Fleming's fingerprints were found on the gun. She informed us that her father bought the gun for her. She adamantly told the police they didn't have a case against her. The police will let a jury decide. Mr. Fleming was there when we arrested his wife. He looked shocked. I imagine this will cause a shakeup at your company."

Ali took Grant's extended hand. She held on tight. "My job isn't important to me. The attack changed my perspective. I planned on quitting soon. My husband and I have other plans in our future."

Detective Moon watched the two lovers.

"Good for you. We're glad to find you once again safe. The police have concluded their investigation around the cabin and outer buildings. We'll be leaving, too. You can get back to a normal existence."

Grant stood and was relieved the interview was over.

The Evans thanked the detectives who left in the rental car for their flight. Matlock permanently moved into the garage and outbuilding as a hired security guard, horse feeder, and general contractor.

Grant squeezed Ali's hand.

"You didn't tell the detectives that you want to become pregnant and we are trying hard."

"No, there are some things too private to tell."

"We should decide on a room for the nursery."

"I've already ordered paint and a frilly bassinet."

"Frilly? Do boys like frilly?"

"No. We can always change the room."

Grant kissed her.

"I like frilly. She can have your hair and eyes and my smarts."

Ali laughed. Their family would get off to a good start. She hoped they would know soon. There were no birth control pills for six months. The doctor told her pregnancy takes its own time.

The delivery truck driver rang the bell.

Three large boxes were placed inside the front door.

"The baby furniture arrived. Do we have any tools in the house?"

"No, I'll get them from the garage."

Ali went to the mailbox and saw a folder addressed to her from her company. She read the note.

Opening the inside folder were ten 8x10 photos. They were the proofs. Ali looked at the photos and smiled. The dress was swirled around the snow and the raven looked good in her hands.

She heard a noise and looked toward a large pinyon tree. A large raven sat looking at her.

"Shiny raven, you are free to go. The killer's name is *Never More*."

The large bird lifted in the air and flew away.

Ali went back inside and started drawing the large raven she saw. When her husband appeared with the tool bag, she showed him her drawing. Then she showed him the photo shoot.

Grant selected one to take to New York. Ali looked beautiful. The picture had special meaning. Without the photo shoot, they wouldn't have gotten back together.

Ali threw the stained pink and white handkerchief in the fireplace. The cloth quickly burned. There was no longer any need to keep the cloth. The detectives showed her a picture of Hector. She didn't know him or remember him. It would take her a while to forgive Lisa and the terrible damage she created.

"The earth is a better place with evil dead or locked away."

She thought about Emily Blunt. Justice was getting a chance to try Mrs. Fleming.

Grant came back into the room. He looked pleased with himself.

"Come look at the pieces. I arranged them exactly like your drawing."

Ali saw the room.

"The nursery furniture fits perfectly."

Grant said, "Did you notice the sign when you went to the mailbox?"

"No, our names have been added? Let's go see."

Ali touched the new carving.

Grant took her hand and they went into their home. Words weren't necessary between them. He knew the sign looked amazing.

## 35 Next Morning's Raven

Ali went out the front door of the cabin the next morning. She brought her camera and was hoping to catch a glimpse of the raven in the pinyon tree. There was no bird there. She took several photographs of the cabin and circular drive in the morning light. She liked the way the shadows looked with the pots and bushes.

Suddenly she heard the raven's caw. The raven flew to a top branch and sat there looking at Ali. She tried talking to the bird in soothing tones. There was no response.

Ali turned to go back into the house. The raven flew to a bush next to the door. There was something red in its mouth. Ali stepped closer. The bird didn't fly away.

"Hello, raven, why are you carrying a red piece of cloth. Oh, my, it's the netting from the scarf at the photo shoot. How did you ever acquire such a piece? It looks dirty. You can't be the same bird. But here you are at my front door. Of course, you flew away when the sheriff opened Hector's motel room. That was a brave move except now you are hungry."

Ali took off her leather belt and wrapped it around the same arm the raven sat at the shoot. She lifted her arm.

"Come."

The raven dropped the red netting and picked it up again.

"Come, raven."

The raven looked at her. Ali felt silly talking to a bird.

"The day was dark and super dreary. Let me see if I can remember more. The night was very cold. You knew a woman previously died. You tapped or used your bill to knock. You were smart and talked."

The raven didn't move.

"I guess your owner wasn't into poems. Poems weren't a favorite subject for a mastermind killer. Who wants to be called deader than dead? How silly? You are here once more."

Ali saw the bird cock his head. She remembered that she spoke at the photo shoot. Somehow the bird was listening to her. Her words were holding the bird in a spell.

"I'm obviously not trained in how to do this bird training or talking. You will have to help me, pretty boy."

The raven reacted and nodded his head.

Ali grinned and clapped because she knew the bird's name. She danced in a little circle.

The raven fluffed its wings acknowledging the dance as something good.

"I'm glad you are delighted with me. I know your name. Let's see if you will come to me like you did once before. Or I guess you didn't exactly come. A handler put you on my arm or was it my shoulder? Good heavens, I can't remember. We must give your name a go. I'm talking in riddles. Sorry. I have things together now. You know the thing is that we must do something. We must try your name."

The raven solemnly looked at the woman.

"Pretty boy, come." Ali lifted her arm.

The black feathered raven lifted and lightly dropped on her leather arm. The raven dropped the netting on her shoulder.

Ali touched the piece and handed the fabric back to the raven.

"You keep the netting. I know the fabric was beautiful and shiny once upon a time. Perhaps you can use the piece in a nest next spring with some female. I would like that very much. I'm glad you flew over the pinyons. They are a good place to hide."

The raven bobbed his head, picked up the netting, and flew off to his tree.

Ali slowly went into the cabin and told Grant her wonderful encounter. Grant called his friend, Red. Red brought a person who owned a rescued bird sanctuary. They placed the meat and water in a large cage. The raven looked at the two men leerily.

Ali stepped in. "Come, pretty boy. It's time to go to a new place. I will promise to visit."

She picked up a piece of meat and held the morsel in her hand. The raven flew to her and she gently lowered him into the cage while he chewed his lunch.

Ali was sad to see the raven go but knew in her heart, the new owners would take good care of the bird. All thoughts regarding her killer were forgotten. She didn't need to try to remember the day of the attack. Her brain blocked the view. Detective Moon gave her a card of a local psychologist. She knew her friends helped her over the hard part.

Grant called Ali and she gladly went into his arms. They would take the helicopter out today and he would show her where they would put the cattle fences. She would need to buy cowboy boots. He would wait to show her plans to expand the cabin.

## 36 Alessandria and Wolf

**The strawberry jam** was cooled enough to put in pint jars for the freezer. She gave up on using the smaller jam jars which didn't seem to last long enough. Five jars fit nicely on the shelf and the last jar was left on the counter. The artisan bread loaves were cooled. She put one in a plastic bag and put the package in their wooden bread box. The second one she packaged and grabbed the labels. Matlock's name was placed on the jar and bread. He would be over later to pick up his present.

Ali finished cleaning the dishes when, suddenly, the doorbell rang. There were no worker people scheduled for the day. The harvest of pinyon nuts was over.

Ali took off her apron and wondered who was at their door. She looked through the peephole and quickly texted Grant the visitor's name before she opened the door.

"Alessandria, isn't it? You must be out shopping for items in your gallery. How nice of you to stop by."

Alessandria walked into the cabin and sat down on the large couch. She seemed wooden to Ali who suddenly wasn't sure what to do. Ali went into the kitchen to make coffee. She hung her apron in the closet. Her visitor followed the owner into the kitchen.

"Do you like your coffee black, cream, or sugar?"

The visitor didn't answer. Ali shakily poured two cups of the hot coffee and put one cup close to the silent woman who was looking at the pots.

"I bought those pots. They are truly ancient and beautiful. The reason I took so much time in finding them is because Grant and I could spend more time together. He was lonely and single. There was no ring on his finger to stop our forward motion. Grant was better than the other ranch owners. He was good looking and rich. Those last two items were of major importance for a woman. Wouldn't you agree?"

Ali waited. She didn't know how to respond.

"I believed Grant would want me to live here. Marriage would eventually follow. You disappeared from his life and I was glad. Then there was the attack in Aspen. The media said you disappeared again. Grant wished he could rescue you. My wish was for you to be dead. Yet, here you are in my place."

Ali swallowed her fear. She was in worst situations than this one. Ali reminded herself to stop the brain freeze. The woman in front of her was obviously a tad demented. Her husband, Grant was on his way into town to pick up his wedding ring that was resized. She wondered how quickly he would return. She needed to keep talking with the visitor to calm her down.

"I'm sorry you feel that way. I didn't know you cared about Grant other than as a client."

"That's right. He was my client. Mine."

Ali was astounded by the anger in the woman's voice. She was glad to see Alessandria drink some coffee. Ali did the same.

"Your kitchen smells like bread and jam. I suppose Grant's maid, Marie, made those before she left. The kitchen feels homey."

Ali didn't want to tell her that she made the bread.

"Marie makes wonderful bread."

"You're alone today?"

Ali wasn't sure if she should answer.

"I have some bread and jam for Matlock. He's around the ranch and knows the present is ready."

Alessandria fingered the bread package. The jam jar held twine wrapped around the rim in a bow for decoration. She touched the twine.

"Where's Grant? I'd like to speak to him about something private."

"Grant went to town and should return shortly. I'm sorry you missed him."

Ali worried about the completed lettering on their raven sign out front. The sign read Ali and Grant Evans Cabin.

Alessandria looked more upset. Ali waited.

"A friend of mine told me there was an announcement and picture in the newspaper. My friend lives in the area. She said you and Grant were married. Is that true?"

"Yes, we were married some time ago. I've known Grant a long time. The attack brought us closer."

Alessandria tapped her spoon on the counter.

"The cowboy came to your rescue."

"Yes, Grant did. He would help anyone of his friends."

Finally, Alessandria said, "He only married you out of pity. I know him well. He would have gotten over you."

Ali filled her cup and put some sugar cinnamon into the brew. She held up the jar to her visitor who shook her head.

"I wish that I could help you resolve some issues about your feelings for Grant. There might have been pity at first with regards to my missing. I did contact Grant. However, our friendship turned into love. The love was there all along. Neither one of us were surprised. I do have a card someone gave me for a therapist. I can get you the card."

"Love, huh! He can't love you. I don't need nor want your help. I want you to leave."

Ali placed her coffee cup in the sink. The woman made her mad. She was angry with Grant for not being there to handle the woman.

"I love my husband. He wants our relationship. We complete each other. Both of us believe the stars have aligned. There is a perfect balance that exists between us. The raven brought us together. We married for better and for worse. I'm not leaving, and I will not break my promise. My husband feels the same way.

You need to leave our home. I'm asking politely. The third time I speak, you will be facing a gun. Get out."

"What raven? I don't believe you that Grant could want you. I've been here. He needs to see me. By the way, what happened to the second time?"

Ali said, "Grant is out of your hemisphere. He hasn't called you for nine months. I skipped the second count. You've put me in a bad mood."

Alessandria picked up the chili jar container and looked at the dried peppers. She put the silver lid on the counter.

Ali moved closer to where the gun was stored in the kitchen. Somehow the silver lid was important to victory. There was no way Ali was relinquishing victory to this trespasser in her home. Trespassers were foreigners per Sheriff Cray and Matlock. Alessandria was trespassing.

Alessandria threw the jar which bounced on the rug and hit the tile floor smashing the glass. The chili peppers flew in disarray on the tile floor. Then she picked up a piece of glass in her hand. The sharpness cut the hand, but she didn't drop the piece.

Now Ali was very alarmed.

"Alessandria stay where you are. Don't move. I'm going to get you some bandages. You are bleeding and in danger. We must get you to see a doctor. Did you hear me?"

The bleeding woman nodded.

Ali left the room. When she came back, she took the glass piece, threw it in the sink, and wrapped the woman's hands with gauze. She steered her visitor out the door into the parked red SUV.

Ali said, "I need the keys. I'm driving you to the hospital."

Alessandria motioned toward the visor. She was mesmerized by the amount of blood in the gauze.

Ali told her to put pressure on the wound. The woman didn't move. Ali unclicked the purse strap and handed the item to her.

"Wrap the strap in your hand. Do it now Alessandria."

The woman wrapped the strap.

"Am I going to die?"

"Let's hope not. We're almost there. Two more lights and we can park in the emergency area."

Alessandria was beginning to realize how afraid she was.

Grant and Matlock arrived at the cabin at the same time. Grant saw Ali's text and turned his vehicle around. He was worried about the two women's encounter. The two men raced into the cabin. They saw the glass and blood in the kitchen and searched the house.

Fear grew in Grant's eyes until he heard his phone ring.

"Ali, thank god, where are you? There's glass and blood."

She told him the two women were at the emergency room. The two men raced to the hospital emergency entrance and found Ali talking to a doctor.

Relief spread over Grant who took his wife into his arms.

"I'm all right. The glass broke and she needed a doctor. I drove Alessandria here and have talked with the doctor. They will take care of her now. We can go home."

Matlock rode in the Evans vehicle. At the cabin he grabbed his present and left the two lovers alone in their world. He was surprised about Alessandria's actions. No one saw her anger and rage heightening.

Later that evening, Ali told Grant what happened.

"I wish that I handled things differently with Alessandria."

"You couldn't know her feelings of desperation. I believe the shock of knowing we married tipped the scale. It's good that she agreed to getting professional help."

Grant was solemn.

"We need to take a honeymoon someplace quiet. My nerves are shot."

"I know the perfect place," said Ali.

"Good. We can start packing tomorrow."

Grant went into the kitchen, removed glass, and cleaned the floor. He didn't tell Ali about the wolf Matlock caught in a trap by the tail. Matlock released the animal. The two men agreed the wolf was not endangering the horses. They would give the animal a second chance.

Two weeks later Ali and Grant were able to leave the cabin. On the way to the airport, they stopped at the jewelry store.

Ali placed the ring on Grant's finger while they were in the vehicle.

"I love you."

Granted kissed his beautiful wife, "I love you back."

Ali breathed a sigh of relief that her husband now wore a real wedding band on his finger. The platinum was a symbol of their love and a warning to other women to stay away. She didn't want to go through another scene like what happened with Alessandria. Grant agreed with her.

"Strange women are considered trespassers."

Ali squeezed his arm as he pulled away to drive to the airport and their honeymoon.

## 37 Detectives on Vacation

**Detective Moon watched** Detective Constantine swim in the pool at their hotel. They planned their vacation together in the Caribbean. Candace put strings attached to her being there. Doug agreed no newspaper, computer, or cell phone until they were back in Los Angeles. He didn't have a problem with the terms except he missed his game app. Being with Candace was better than the app. He swam over to her lounge chair and hoisted his body out of the warm pool water.

"You look better in a bikini than your detective outfit."

"You look better, too. I'm thirsty. I ordered us pink lemonade."

Doug's face fell.

"The lemonade is good for you, especially in this hot sun. Our bodies are important. We must keep hydrated."

They both were quiet watching the other guests.

"I thought we could drive around the island later and go exploring. One of the hotel employees told me there are a bunch of tourist shops on the east side. He told me there were some interesting shells around the island. They offer shell carving classes. We might try a fun class."

"I need to swim a little bit first."

# RAIMENT RED AND A RAVEN

The two detectives played frisbee in the water and floated around the deep end.

On the drive to the shops, they slowed the car to let some geese cross the road. Candace laughed.

"Canada. Do you think they followed us from Canada?"

"Naw. Vancouver's too far."

Coming back to the hotel loaded with shells and straw hats, they went to the local restaurant for dinner.

The next three days was more relaxation, riding on scooters to the top of the island, and sailing around the inner harbor. After three days of eating seafood, they decided to eat in their room the last evening.

Doug was eating barley soup and Candace had a large salad. The pile of newspapers sat on their hotel desk.

Doug deposited them in the garbage.

"We won't be needing these. Did you see they brought me a jelly donut?"

"I noticed right away. They must have been out of cinnamon."

"No, there's pineapple inside. I like pineapple and the fruit is good for you."

Candace smiled. She picked up a piece of hard-boiled egg and held the morsel in her teeth.

"I should have told you no eggs on this trip. But I'm a nice guy."

"You are a nice guy. Maybe we can go to Vancouver for our next vacation."

"Now you're talking."

They spent their last night together and eventually boarded the airplane. Both of their faces were sunburned and content. Romance was a normal step after working closely together. The case was a difficult one to crack and they spent many nights talking. Candace fell asleep on the plane on the return flight. Doug removed his cell phone from his pocket and looked at the game app. He thought better of playing the device and put the phone in his pocket.

Next morning, they would drink coffee together at a local coffee shop. They liked the different selections of brew. Candace stirred her vanilla latte. Doug drank his double coffee. They read the newspapers left on the table.

"Holy smokes, you have to read this article. We missed something important while we were on vacation."

Candace read the headlines, "The jury acquitted Mrs. Fleming of all charges in the murder of Emily Lund. I don't understand."

The two detectives read the article together.

Candace said, "Her attorney was clever in showing the gun contained many fingerprints. Some of the fingerprints were her grandfather's, the maid, Mr. Fleming, and a few unknown. The fabric was a common nylon used for winter garments at the time. Per Mrs. Fleming's testimony, they stuffed a scarecrow with straw and dressed the dummy. The dummy wore the same nylon fabric as Emily's jacket. Mrs. Fleming used the dummy for target shooting as did the rest of the employees and guests at the house. The guest list was longer when the family went on a fox hunt at their estate acreages. Mrs. Fleming kept the gun because of sentimental reasons. The gun was kept in her tea cart drawer for years. She forgot about owning the gun until someone stole the object from her home. She divulged this information prior to her arrest to two detectives. Mrs. Fleming was innocent and never tried to hide things from the police."

Doug and Candace wondered at the flimsiness of their case.

"I thought we had things pretty nailed down. It just goes to show you how wrong we were. Their lawyer tore through the evidence. There was a solid block and then the block became swiss cheese. She made us look like idiots."

"Loopholes, we call them loopholes. I like cheese."

Candace was trying to figure something out. "I'm not sure we were wrong."

"What are you thinking?"

"I called the Flemings house to speak to the maid. She's no longer employed there. Don't you think that's unusual? She's kept most of her staff for years. Why would she get rid of Consuelo Santos?"

"Maybe she retired."

"Consuelo told me she was forty-five years old and liked her job. Could she have seen someone or something?"

"Do we know where to find Consuelo?"

"She's living with her daughter in an apartment in Albuquerque. Consuelo works in a rug shop in the city. We'll need to wait until she is done working. In the meantime, I think we should try to find silver belt buckles. There's a place next to one of the shops that sells the leather to go with the buckle."

"I was hoping you would say Canada. I'm tired of flying into the same city repeatedly. I've tried everything in their food machines at the airport. The buckles sound interesting."

"Poor, Doug. I'll make sure we eat at a nice Mexican restaurant when we go there. We'll be downtown and there are many eateries."

"Good. Then when do you want me to get the airplane tickets?"

"Let me see if Mrs. Fleming will see us?"

Doug believed his partner was pushing her luck. A few days later, they were on an airplane. Candace was prepared for the interview with Consuelo and carried several photographs in her briefcase.

The Flemings refused to see the detectives. They were not in the area. The Flemings were on a ship in Europe on vacation.

## 38 Former Maid

**The detectives waited** until Consuelo Santos was done working. Consuelo wore a gold uniform dress, carried her market bag, and sat down at their table. The detectives introduced themselves and they ordered tacos.

"This is the best place for tacos. The owners will allow us to eat and talk. They told me we can stay at our table as long as we want."

"Thank you for checking with them. What do you recommend?"

"The dish of the day is always good."

Doug ordered the pork tamales and Candace ordered the chicken soft tacos.

When their coffee was brought to the table, Candace took charge of the interview.

"Consuelo, you have worked for Mrs. Fleming for eight years. As the maid, your duties were to deliver food and drink from the kitchen for Mrs. Fleming's guests and her bridge club."

"Yes. Sometimes Mr. Fleming required my services. Most of the time, my work was involved in helping his wife. Wednesday was her hairdresser day."

"Did Mrs. Fleming indicate why your services were no longer needed?"

"She told me some of her guests complained about me. I was told Mrs. Fleming would give me three month's wages to allow me to find another job. She would give me a fair reference. So, I came to live with my daughter."

"You were employed at the house during the attack on Lisa Givens and Ali Zarin?"

"Yes, such a terrible waste for those two women."

"Do you read the newspapers or the television?"

"No, my reading isn't very good. The English words are hard to remember. I don't watch much television. There's too much noise. My daughter goes to her room to view her favorite shows."

"Detective Constantine and I have some photographs to show you. Were any of these people visitors with Mrs. Fleming?"

Consuelo looked at the photographs. Ali and Lisa's photographs were selected. Candace turned the pictures over. She slid the next two photographs. Ms. Santos selected one photograph.

"He came with Lisa Givens one time together. The man came again. I believe he was there four times. Mrs. Fleming always saw guests on her bridge day which was Tuesday. I could never have Tuesdays off."

Doug slid over his computer and explained her signature was required to go with her statement. Consuelo signed with her finger.

"I won't get in trouble with Mrs. Fleming for talking with you."

Candace looked at Doug.

"No. It's always important to tell the truth. You've done a good thing by talking with us. The rich sometimes feel they are exempt from the law. Our job is to search for facts. The facts will be used to push for justice."

Consuelo nodded.

"Mrs. Fleming might still be in trouble."

Doug smiled.

The detectives thanked Ms. Santos. Detective Moon asked Consuelo if she's ever worked for any of the ranches in the area.

"I did a long time ago. I don't know too many ranchers."

Detective Moon handed her a name. Consuelo looked at the card.

"Grant Evans?"

"The sheriff for the area told me the ranch is expanding and are looking for a general housekeeper and light cook to fill in when their other maid is unavailable. He told me they pay well and are planning to increase the ground buildings at several of their property locations."

"Thank you, detectives. I will watch for their ad in the newspaper. My daughter may be interested."

The detectives went back to their hotel room. Their next step was to recover phone records.

Doug took Candace in his arms.

"We should be over with this case soon."

"I know. Hector's paper calendar was enlightening. Good catch reading his book at the evidence room when we returned from vacation. The police put his belongings from the motel in the evidence room. We went through those boxes. Another box came later from his desk at Wilderness Farms. The calendar was in that box. I'm sure he didn't need the book anymore and wasn't concerned about leaving the item behind."

"The evidence guy knows us. He called me about the second box. I gave him tickets to a hockey game. Do we know when the Flemings will return home?"

"They should be back next month. This is critical that we keep our investigation quiet. I don't want Mrs. Fleming to disappear."

"Why do you think she became involved?"

"Who knows a person's motives? Perhaps Lisa's pregnancy rocked her cocoon world."

"Mr. Fleming wasn't the father."

"She doesn't know those facts. We were smooth about not revealing our sneaky DNA trick."

Doug sat down in the hotel room chair.

"Let's stroll around downtown and clear our heads. I'm ready to look at silver buckles. I'm thinking arrows would look good as a design."

"What about wolves?"

Doug steered her into the first shop. The clerk approached the two lovers. Doug told the clerk, "No wolves. They're too scary. Besides they remind me too much of my job."

The clerk showed them various designs. Doug picked a horse with inlaid turquoise arrows. Candace picked a group of horses running with a gold trim. They went next door and purchased their leathers. They found a blue jean's shop and bought a new pair.

Laughingly they tried on cowboy boots and couldn't decide.

"I like my tennis shoes best. However, those leather short boots might be worth a trip back."

"I'll buy you the boots for finding the calendar."

Doug brightened.

"I'll buy you a silver and turquoise ring just cause."

"You're on. Whoa, wait a minute. The ring doesn't mean anything special?"

Doug took her hand, "Don't be silly. I know how to propose and I'm not ready. I have to save some more money."

"I have money."

"We do need to talk about our money. First, we get this case out of our heads."

"I can wait."

They went into a shop and bought her ring. The boot shop was surprised to see the couple return. There was only fifteen minutes before the shop closed. Doug walked outside with his box of boots in a plastic bag. The couple ran to their vehicle when large drops fell from the sky.

"This is crazy weather we're having. Let's hope the rain is gone by morning when we catch our flight."

Candace looked at the silver ring on her finger. The shape was a flower rimmed in gold.

## 39 Flashing Lights

**The police pulled** into the Flemings opulent estate in the hills of Los Angeles with their lights flashing. There were no sirens. The neighbors looked out large front windows and pulled their drapes. Friends quickly exit when trouble knocks next door.

Detective Moon and Detective Constantine rang the doorbell. The new maid let them into the house. The police waited outside.

Mrs. Fleming hurriedly came to the entry hall. She didn't have time to unpack her bags.

"What is the meaning of this intrusion? You are not wanted here. Gene, order them to go away."

Gene Fleming walked into the hall.

"I believe the officers are at our door for a reason. We can at least listen to their story. Please come into the living room."

"Thank you, Mr. Fleming. We do have some information that has arisen while you were on vacation. I'm sorry you haven't had the time to unpack. We wanted to be sure the family was staying home."

"What could be so important that you scared our neighbors with police lights?"

Mrs. Fleming sat rigid in her chair. She waived the new maid off. There would be no tea and sandwiches.

Candace held several copies of the pages from Hector Hansen's calendar and placed them on the coffee table. Mrs. Fleming glanced at the handwriting and dates.

Mr. Fleming said, "I don't understand. The pages look like someone's calendar."

Candace put Consuelo Santos signed statement on the table.

Mrs. Fleming picked the document up and read the statement. She handed the document to her husband who read the paper.

"Hector Hansen was a guest in my home," angrily responded Mr. Fleming.

He turned to his wife. "You knew the killer? Are you insane?"

"So, I knew the man. Lisa brought him here. She wanted me to meet the birdman. That's not a crime."

"Your initials are on one of the dates."

"I saw the MF. Those could be your initials."

Mr. Fleming's face turned red.

"They can't be my initials. I never knew the man. Nor did I ever see him until there was a dead body in the news."

Doug looked at Candace.

"Mr. Fleming. You might want to get a lawyer."

"I need a lawyer?"

"No, sir, your wife does."

Mr. Fleming sat down. There was no response from Mrs. Fleming. She was cold as black onyx stone.

Doug thought of a black wolf. He nodded to his partner to continue.

Detective Moon brought out the travel brochures of Ben's trips and a travel brochure from Acapulco.

"Mrs. Fleming used Fun Time Travel to make vacation plans for Ben Blake and one time for Latin Dooley. She paid for Ben's travel because he knew about her gun and silencer. Ben made the mistake of asking her to make Latin's travel plans."

"I liked Ben and felt my husband didn't pay him enough in bonuses. There is no crime in making travel arrangements."

Mr. Fleming looked at his wife as if she was a total stranger. He opened his mouth and shut it again.

Detective Moon took out her recorder.

"There's a recording of a phone call you both need to listen. The recording was made to Mrs. Fleming the day before Hector Hansen went on the rampage to kill Ali Zarin."

She pushed the play button. They heard a dial tone and the phone was picked up. There was silence and the sound started.

*"I've found Ali Zarin."*

*The woman on the other line said, "I'm glad my information was accurate."*

*"I can leave, or I can finish this job."*

*"I don't care."*

*The woman hung up the phone as did the man.*

Mr. Fleming stood up and left the room. He was making a phone call.

The detectives watched Mrs. Fleming for a reaction. There was none.

"Mrs. Fleming, you were the mastermind."

The woman didn't answer.

Mr. Fleming quickly came down the stairs with his briefcase and suitcase. The detectives let him proceed to the door. He was not the person they were at the home to arrest. Mr. Fleming stopped and pointed his finger at his wife.

"You killed Lisa Givens. Why? She was pregnant."

"That's exactly why, you egotistical, screwball of a husband. I've cleaned up your messes. I'm the one who fixed things so you could play."

Her husband came closer to his wife and then thought better of it. Her hatred was not any part of him.

"Gene, where are you going?"

"I've called my lawyer and he is preparing divorce papers. I will not let you drag me down. You'll need to find your own lawyer."

"You can't divorce me. What about my money?"

"Money won't save you. I'm sorry detectives. I appreciate all your help. You have my lawyer's name and he will know where to contact me. I'm leaving this hellish woman and her house. I'll make sure the victim's families are compensated. This is California and I know the laws. Good day."

Mr. Fleming walked out of the house and drove away.

"Do you have anything you would like to say before we invite the police in to arrest you," said Doug. Both he and Detective Moon stood up.

"There's a perfect explanation for my knowing Mr. Hansen. You detectives have lost your marbles and are on the wrong course again. The only difference this time is that I will need to get a different lawyer."

Candace couldn't believe the woman.

"You've destroyed people and screwed with their lives. Prison is too nice a place for you, Mrs. Fleming. If things were up to me, I wouldn't use a gun or a trip wire. I'd throw your body off the nearest cliff."

"How dare you talk to me this way?"

Doug went to the front door and let the police inside. He would never forget the look on Mrs. Fleming's face as the officers put her in the police vehicle.

The maid came back into the room.

Detective Moon told her the house would be busy with police the rest of the day. She could probably take a vacation. The maid delightedly left the room.

"Well, Sherlock, this arrest was a little too exciting."

Detective Moon put her evidence copies and tape recorder into her briefcase.

Doug said, "I didn't think she would confess, but she said some words that were mighty close. I doubt a jury will believe her this time. Also, her husband has pulled the plug, or should we say drapes."

"I saw the neighbors. How rude?"

Detective Constantine was glad she was back. Sometimes cases were a downer. Doug handed her a ball of yellow paper.

"Ugh, gum."

They walked out to the main driveway and talked with their boss.

"Nice job, Detective Moon and Constantine. We thought we were going to have to storm the place until Mr. Fleming came out. He seemed like a nice person. I like the news company and watch every chance I get. It's too bad about his wife. Not every day your wife turns out to be a murderer and accomplice. Her husband walked out with dignity. I've got to get back to the office. The phones will be ringing off the hook with reporter questions."

Candace and Doug strolled down the street where their car was parked.

"I like the beach view in between the houses. There's a nice beach down the road. Do you have any quarters for the meters?"

She brought out a roll and handed the brown paper to him.

They walked the beach until sundown. They drove to a restaurant in a hotel and ate an expensive meal.

"Are you feeling better?"

"Yes. There's a calm feeling when a person sits by the ocean."

"The boss told me earlier we don't have to report to our desk tomorrow. Which hotel do you want to stay in tonight?"

"This one."

"I'll go make the arrangements."

Detective Moon waited near the piano in the lobby. The music drifted inside and outside the hotel. This was the way life was supposed to be.

Murder was not the normal in most people's lives. Sheriff Cray warned her about the fallout of the job. He told her criminals were trespassers more dangerous than any wolf. She liked his comparison but felt the wolf was getting a bad rap. She didn't consider the criminals fallout. Dangerous was their name only when they held power.

"They really are more like Doug's comment. Criminals can be stupid."

She sent Sheriff Cray a text message. "You were right. We caught her. The old file raised awareness on a major scale."

Sheriff Cray responded, "The entire police force here thanks you."

A waiter brought her a glass of champagne.

"Courtesy of the house, maam."

"Oh, in that case, can I have one for my friend. He's extra special."

The waiter put down a second glass and napkin.

"Enjoy your evening."

Candace was going to reply but the waiter moved on to the other hotel guests.

Doug sat down and handed her the reservation and room keys.

"They sell clothes in one of the shops or we could use bathrobes in the room."

"Are they big bathrobes?"

"Hey, champagne. Good deal. What's with the bathrobes question?"

"Let's go to our room and I'll show you."

Doug grinned.

"Okay, partner."

Candace called the spa and ordered a fragrant oil delivered to their room. She knew how to play.

# 40 Barbeque Reception

**Mr. and Mrs. Evans** were delighted to see their entire ranch road and field were filled with cars and trucks. There were two barbeque areas drawing the crowd of people. One area was a large pit with pig and the other was a large grill with steaks. There were two food trucks delivering cheese and vegetable tacos and the other truck fruit and chocolate tacos.

There were tables and chairs from the rental company spread on large heavy tarps under white tents. White balloons and white flowers adorned the tent area. Huge black bows were tied to the white covered chairs. Grey buckets of ice were on the tables with small bottles of wine. The beer kegs were in another tent filled with cowboys and musicians playing soft Mexican music.

Sheriff Cray was talking to Detective Moon and Constantine when Ali approached them. Her hair was tied back in curls and she wore a white satin pant suit with black silk over blouse. The blouse was pleated in front with lace. Grant was on her heels in the reverse attire. He wore black attire with a white silk shirt. There were new cowboy boots with black and silver on both their feet.

"This shindig of yours is stellar. Where'd you get them boots? They don't have boots in New York City?

"Yes, we found them in New York City."

Matlock approached the couple.

"Congratulations to two of my best friends. I also noticed the boots."

Grant shook Matlock's hand and Matlock hugged Ali.

"You get prettier every day," said Matlock.

"Don't worry, Ali, he uses the same line on my wife," said Sheriff Cray.

"Those boots look mighty fancy and expensive." Matlock touched the silver tips.

"Can't you see the boots are real nice cow leather, and they might last on a trail ride," argued Sheriff Cray.

Grant and Ali turned to escape Matlock and the sheriff's argument regarding boots.

"Thank you for coming. We're trying to talk to all our guests except the going is slow. Have a good time. Oh, Sheriff, your wife is talking to the guitar player and they are swapping recipes."

"By golly, I better go intervene or there won't be any more music the rest of the night. Excuse me, everyone," said Sheriff Cray.

Detective Moon laughed at the banter among the ranch friends.

"Ali, I like your style very much. This barbeque reception is the most fun we've had in a long time."

"You're welcome. I see George and Mr. Johnson are here with Milan and Laila. I need to talk with them. I also wanted to thank you for Consuelo. Grant and I like her and her daughter very much. They will be moving to our cabin in the pinyons. We'll need a babysitter for our daughter."

Detective Moon was delighted. She could see Grant was still hanging tight to Ali.

"Congratulations. We wish you the best. Let us know when there will be a baby shower. We'd love to fly in again."

Detective Constantine rolled his eyes. He thought they were done flying into Albuquerque. Candace nudged him in the ribs.

Ali talked with George.

"How's Miss Kitty?"

"Pregnant. Tom cat came by our house when we weren't watching. One litter, my dad told me. Do you want a kitty? Maybe Matlock, too."

"I'd like a kitty very much. Now, go enjoy the chocolate ice cream tacos. We skipped the cake at the barbeque this time."

"I can wait for cake. I like white cake with strawberry," said George. He and his father moved toward the food trucks.

Milan and Laila were holding hands.

Grant noticed his friend from the cabin, Red Drake, and his wife, Lara, weren't there. Grant gave them a quick call on his cell phone.

He came back to the group. "I'm glad your mom and dad can make the barbeque, Laila. They called to say they will be late. They mentioned something about bringing a good luck charm."

Laila smiled. "They ordered a wooden horse made with a raven carved on the rump. I probably shouldn't have told you. Therefore, you must act surprised. The horse is child size. A friend in Santa Fe makes the toys. The raven will hold a branch with red berries. My mother was given one of Ali's drawings. The artist used Ali's design."

"We'll be surprised."

Grant steered Ali toward the ranch casita and unlocked the door. They went inside.

"Whew, I'm bushed from shaking hands. Can we go back to Hawaii? The ranch grounds are filled with people and cops. The police are wearing their guns."

"You know you love the barbeque. Everyone in town will be talking about us for months. The police wear their guns all the time. I'm sure the detectives are carrying as is Matlock. A barbeque is a normal day for them. Their guns will keep everyone in line."

"I'm afraid you are right."

Grant looked at his wife. He was proud of her coordinating the barbeque. The food trucks and fireworks were her idea.

"Come here sweet woman. We have privacy for a few minutes. Did I tell you today, I love you?"

"Yes, you did. I believe we have ten minutes before people realize we are missing. The kisses happened before breakfast, during breakfast, and after breakfast. There's now and I'm not sure how many more times before the evening is through."

"There will be much more."

Grant kissed her on the lips and Ali kissed her husband back. Their life was falling neatly into place.

"If one more woman asks me how many carats are in my diamond ring, I'm going to lie."

"No, honey, you need to tell them you lost count after three."

"I can't do that, they'll think I'm a snob cowgirl."

"Have you looked at your new cowgirl boots? They cost a small fortune."

"My cowboy bought them for me. He's to blame. He is a smooth talker."

"Oh, no, you don't. I'm okay with the cowboy part. You're to blame for coming back and twisting my heart beyond all repair."

"I take the heart blame. I should confess that I was ready to leave the shine of LA lights for silver-tipped boots and a rock."

"Ali, come here."

Grant touched her silk-satin outfit in all the right places. His wife groaned.

"You're too smooth. I don't care what you tell anybody at the barbeque as long as you are staying in my arms."

"I'm staying for a long time, sweetheart."

The two lovers kissed and were making the kiss last longer than a three-carat rock and silver-tipped boots.

They heard the key turn in the lock and Milan came into the house. He asked Laila to wait outside for him.

Ali said, "There goes our ten minutes."

"Milan, is there a problem with the barbeque?"

"We're out of beer. There are three well done steaks left and a little pork. Matlock is eying the steaks. But most people have moved to the dessert truck and the coffee urns. The iced tea has been a hit. The children used all the peach syrup and ate the maraschino cherries. The fireworks crew are setting their gear in the ground. They'll let me know when they are ready to ignite. The firemen arrived five minutes ago. Once the fireworks are ready, I'll round the guest mob and station them outside the tents."

Grant told him, "Go find Matlock, he hid a couple kegs of beer in the garage. He and the Sheriff can find some boys to help move the kegs. They're next to the dynamite. Tell the cook to let Matlock have the steaks and Mrs. Cray can have the pork for tamales. Did the cook put on the chicken pieces? The firemen will be hungry."

Milan shook his head. "I already talked to the cook and he's wrapped the meat in foil. The chicken is cooking. The gravy is getting hot. The pot of corn with peppers tasted mighty fine. There will be enough for the firemen and firework crew."

Milan hesitated.

"What else do we have, Milan?"

"There's something you don't know."

"I don't want to hear about anything strange until tomorrow. Can't you see, I'm trying to have a conversation with my wife."

"No, you're not. I saw you making out and kissing her all over."

"Mind your own business, little brother."

Milan relaxed on the kitchen counter. He wanted to see Grant's face.

"We moved the dynamite. We were worried about the fireworks tonight being a problem. We decided to bury the stuff in the old mine we found on Johnson's ranch. The dynamite is in heavy metal, locked boxes. We stamped the boxes so people would know what was inside. The caves should be cooler than our ranch garage."

"We have an old mine on our Johnson property? I didn't know the mine was there. It's not on any of the maps. I researched the older maps of the area. Where is the mine located?"

"Johnson kept the mine a secret all these years. Even George doesn't know about the mine. Johnson wouldn't tell the oil company either. He figured you would find out soon enough. There's a tree that was in front of the opening. The mine was put in around the 1800's by a couple miners who cut their own timbers. They, obviously, kept their secret when they died. We pruned the tree a little bit to get the boxes inside. Now you can see the rafters from a hundred yards. Remember the large oak tree in the northwest corner?"

"There's the hill, and at one time there was a running water creek. I remember the oak tree. Now, the creek bed is dry and deep."

"That's the spot. Old man Johnson was doing a little prospecting and finding gold."

Grant was alert.

"How much gold?"

Milan was glad they were inside the casita. He still didn't trust that someone might be listening. He whispered the amount of gold in Ali's ear. Ali put her hands over her mouth and laughed. Milan whispered in Grant's ear the same figure.

Grant was cold sober.

Ali whispered in Grant's ear. Grant wrapped Ali in his arms and kissed her passionately.

Milan stopped in his tracks watching the two married people.

Grant surfaced, "If I was an intelligent man, I wouldn't leave my girlfriend waiting outside with handsome and heavily muscled firemen."

Milan looked at the door where he shut Laila out. He scrambled to leave the casita. Milan went outside to an awaiting Laila who was talking with a fireman.

Grant saw the group and locked the door.

"I think we solved his woman problem."

"Do you think we are rich?" asked Ali.

Grant took Ali in his arms. He didn't care about money. The gold could wait.

"Can we do the barbeque and wait a little while before exploring the mine? My life is too exciting right now. I need some time to think how to approach our new problem. We might need some engineering people to assess the damage."

"You think of gold as damage?"

"No, the old timbers, sweetheart. We don't want anyone getting hurt. I like the gold concept. I've always wanted to dig in rock and find a vein of quartz that leads to gold."

"I agree."

"Okay, then let's go outside and watch fireworks with our friends. They should be over in ten minutes. We can dance afterwards when the party winds down."

Ali walked outside with Grant and they disappeared together among the throng of people moving outside the white tents to view the night sky. She knew Grant would tackle their next project later. However, tonight belonged to her and Grant.

The first fireworks started. Ali moved Grant's hand toward her tummy. Their baby girl moved. Grant snuggled her closer.

Ali wasn't afraid any more.

## 41 Sanctuary Release

**The sanctuary called** Mrs. Evans to let her know they were re-releasing the raven she brought into the sanctuary back into the wild. They wanted to release the bird near their cabin if possible.

Ali and Grant were excited when the bird sanctuary people called. The snow melted and the rivers were full of life. Birds were finding mates and making nests.

The raven they brought to the sanctuary was a male. The sanctuary was also given a female from the wild who needed care and medicine. The female got better and was placed next to their raven. Each were in their own cages.

The two ravens seemed enamored with each other. One day, they let them freely fly within the inner sanctuary dome structure. The sanctuary believed the two ravens mated. They would be released together to build a nest and home in two weeks.

Ali called the designer of the red dress she wore in Aspen. She asked if there was any fabric left. The designer mailed Ali a yard of the sheer red fabric. Ali rubbed a foot square of the fabric on her arm and brought the piece outside. The sunlight shone on the piece giving the red hue a magical glow.

Red Drake, their friend, placed the shiny netting in a large tree. The netting was high and inside the tree with a small piece protruding.

Ali hoped the area was where the two ravens would build a nest. The tree was in a grouping of trees past their wooden sign. The grouping of trees would afford the birds privacy from the Evans many visitors.

In two weeks, the sanctuary people arrived with the two cages. The birds were each given the opportunity to catch small desert animals over a month period and to be given branches from trees in the local area that would bear fruit. The fruit they gave the birds was dried. They hoped the smell when the trees burst their fruit would signal memories in the birds.

The two birds could care for themselves and didn't rely on the sanctuary owners other than water and a clean cage. The Evans ranch contained many water sources for the birds and the acreage to fly and live their life free.

The birds were released. The male raven flew to Ali and landed on her shoulder. The female flew to a pinyon tree.

"Hello, pretty boy. I'm very glad to see you have returned with a friend. You will need to hunt for food. I know you are smart and will show her the way. You've been here before and this is now your home. See if you can find my present."

Ali lifted the bird high and dropped her arm. The male raven flew to the stand of trees beyond their sign. She could see him searching. He called to the female raven and she flew inside the tree.

Grant came close to his wife.

"Do you think they found the red netting?"

"Yes. They are in the correct pinyon. We need to leave the ravens alone to find twigs and other items for their nest."

"Not to worry, George and Matlock helped me assemble a bundle of nest stuff on the south end of the horse pasture. We think they will find the new water trough and bundle of nesting we placed there. George brought a dead field mouse and lizard just in case the ravens required a head start. He told us Ms. Kitty caught them."

Ali laughed at Ms. Kitty's contributions.

"Thank you, Grant."

"Ali, your raven is home."

"Correction, our raven family is a part of the Evans family and cabin in the pinyons. Their feathers will fall and rest on the ground. Our children will find them. There will be lots of stories to tell sitting around the fire.

Red Drake handed Ali a ceramic bowl with a lid. The lid handle was a black raven. "My wife, Lara, made this for you on her new pottery wheel. She told me the bowl is a place to put wishes. She's been researching raven designs for our jewelry."

"Thank you, Red. Tell Lara my jar will be in the kitchen window with the herb plants."

"Ali, we believe by untying the raven's legs a long time ago and placing the raven upright in the tree, the raven's spirit was released. The raven could then go back and forth between worlds," said Red Drake.

"Interesting theory. I can use the myth in my stories to our children."

LINDA MCKOWN

Grant watched the two ravens busily check out the tree and talk to each other. He took Ali's hand.

"Our children. You've said the words twice. I like the words and the fact there will be more. We'll tell them about the spirit of the raven and how this one found us."

www.ingramcontent.com/pod-product-compliance
Lightning Source LLC
Chambersburg PA
CBHW062140170626
46813CB00002B/760